What people are

Talking with Angel about Illness, Death and Survival

Honestly, I was very moved by the story's emotional power and the depth of the teachings it conveys. I found the story gripping from the very beginning, but I think what hit me the most was the account Evelyn Elsaesser wrote, in epistolary form, of James' near-death experience. It is simply one of the best and richest accounts (even if it is fiction) of an NDE I've ever come across. I don't think it is saying too much to claim that in itself this bit of writing is a masterpiece.

— **Dr Kenneth Ring**, Professor Emeritus of Psychology, University of Connecticut

This is an accurate and sensitive novel about life after death, written from the perspective of a dying girl. Her discovery of what anyone can now discover, namely the amazing Near-Death-Experience evidence for continued consciousness, will help all readers, old and young, in their approach to what will it seems turn out not to be our final moments. It will move you and it will help teach you how to face death.

— **Dr Lance Butler**, Professor of British literature of the 17th, 18th and 19th centuries, Université de Pau et des Pays de l'Adour, France, Chairman, The Sir Arthur Conan Doyle Centre, Edinburgh, Scotland

From her acknowledged position as one of the world's most well-known researchers and writers on the near-death experience, Evelyn Elsaesser produces an evocative and moving story about dying. Elsaesser's triumph is in providing a genuine resource — not simply for all children and parents desiring education about death and dying, but as one of the few books in the world one can put into the hands of a child who is facing a life-threatening illness.

— **Dr Allan Kellehear**, Professor Emeritus of Palliative Care, University of Bradford, UK

Evelyn Elsaesser has written a beautiful book that I will recommend to my colleagues and, when appropriate, to clients. It is not only well written, but the content is insightful and education. At one point it brought tears to my eyes. I'm confident it will be heartily welcomed by many professionals and non-professionals alike.

— **Dr Louis E. LaGrand**, PhD, CT, Distinguished Service Professor Emeritus at the State University of New York

In this very good and most important and comforting book, Evelyn Elsaesser uses a totally new and emotional approach by confronting the reader with the spiritual lessons to be learned from NDEs by becoming intimately involved in the story of a girl facing leukemia, and her transformation during the progression of her disease.

— **Dr Pim van Lommel**, author of *Near-Death Experience In Survivors of Cardiac Arrest: A Prospective Study in the Netherlands*, The Lancet

Talking with Angel is a courageous book that forces us to confront our worst fears. In the end, however, Evelyn provides us with a sense of hope, a peace of mind, and an invitation into a realm of possibilities that is more beautiful than we can even imagine. *Talking with Angel* is a triumph for the human spirit.

— **Dr Allan Botkin**, author of *Induced After Death Communication: A New Therapy for Healing Grief and Trauma*

With her vast knowledge of NDEs, Elsaesser has succeeded in demonstrating how NDEs can be helpful to those facing

death. Although sad at times, this book highlights the spiritual growth that can be achieved as a result of contemplating one's own mortality. A lovely book, useful for those facing a life-threatening illness, and also for their carers, nurses and doctors.
— **Dr Penny Sartori**, Former Intensive Therapy Unit Nurse, Researcher, Lecturer and Author, UK

Talking with Angel provides an experiential rollercoaster. Reflection on completion of the book enables me fully to appreciate the journey taken by the reader and the spiritual awakening it provoked. This book is for anyone with questions about the fairness of who lives and who dies, or about life after death. It is also for health professionals wishing to engender hope in people who are faced with death. This book will provide valuable insight and wisdom long after it is put back on the shelf.
— **Dr Susanne Becker**, Lecturer in School of Nursing and Midwifery, University of South Australia

Gripping reading. The only other book that it calls to mind is Tolstoy's *The Death of Ivan Ilyich,* although Ivan does not achieve the wisdom displayed in this book. The format is a tour de force. The simplicity of the narrative structure provides the vehicle through which spiritual wisdom is formulated and transmitted in an eminently palatable fashion. Once you read this book you will understand why human life is such a gift and can be passed on to those in need.
— **David Lorimer**, Scientific and Medical Network, Galileo Project

Talking with Angel is a powerful story of a young girl who becomes a woman during her intense struggle with a life-threatening illness. I recommend this book highly to *everyone* who values personal growth and spiritual transformation.
— **Bill Guggenheim**, author of *Hello from Heaven*

I just finished reading *Talking with Angel* this morning, and had a good cry (shame on you for making a grown man cry!) Bravo. It is a wonderful, page turner of a story which imparts the very essence of the NDE without falling into the trap of being overtly expositional. I loved it.
— **Peter Shockey**, Writer / Producer

I have just finished reading your lovely book, *Talking with Angel*, and I certainly found it to be a fascinating and lovely way of describing what you've learned in all your years of studying near-death experiences. I think your book would be very comforting to anyone facing their own death or that of a loved one, and helpful to those seeking to learn more about the NDE experience as well. So I am pleased to recommend it to my clients and colleagues at Hospice of the Valley, as well as to visitors to my Grief Healing Website.
— **Marty Tousley**, APRN, BC, CT, Bereavement Counselor

I consider *Talking with Angel* one of the most powerful and helpful books I have ever read. I am sure it will help countless numbers of people understand and accept their eventual journeys to that wonderful "new dimension" of life that awaits us all.
— **Rev Richard Southworth**, Austin, Texas

Evelyn Elsaesser

Talking with Angel about Illness, Death and Survival

Foreword by Kenneth Ring
Translated into English by Mary Payne

Evelyn Elsaesser

Talking with Angel about Illness, Death and Survival

Foreword by Kenneth Ring
Translated into English by Mary Payne

ROUNDFIRE
BOOKS

Winchester, UK
Washington, USA

JOHN HUNT PUBLISHING

First published by Roundfire Books, 2022
Roundfire Books is an imprint of John Hunt Publishing Ltd., No. 3 East St., Alresford,
Hampshire SO24 9EE, UK
office@jhpbooks.com
www.johnhuntpublishing.com
www.roundfire-books.com

For distributor details and how to order please visit the 'Ordering' section on our website.

ISBN: 978 1 80341 330 3
978 1 80341 331 0 (ebook)
Library of Congress Control Number: 2022911956

A CIP catalogue record for this book is available from the British Library.

Design: Lapiz Digital
Cover image Le Pays d'Ange by Cathy Vial, Les Presses du Midi, Toulon, France

UK: Printed and bound by CPI Group (UK) Ltd, Croydon, CR0 4YY
Printed in North America by CPI GPS partners

We operate a distinctive and ethical publishing philosophy in
all areas of our business, from our global network of authors to
production and worldwide distribution.

Contents

About the Author

Evelyn Elsaesser is an independent researcher and author in the field of death-related experiences, notably Near-Death Experiences (NDEs) and After-Death Communications (ADCs). She has written numerous books, book chapters and papers on these subjects, including *Lessons from the Light*, co-authored with Kenneth Ring.

She is the project leader of the 5-year international research project "Investigation of the Phenomenology and Impact of Spontaneous After-Death Communications (ADCs)" and Founding member and member of the Board of Swiss IANDS (International Association for Near-Death Studies). She lives in Switzerland.

*For the sick children everywhere and for all persons
who will die one day*

Life is eternal;
And love is immortal;
And death is only a horizon;
And a horizon is nothing save the limit of our sight.

Rossiter Worthington Raymond, 1840–1918

Foreword

Plato taught that the whole purpose of philosophy—his dialectic—was to prepare us for death. Nothing, in his view, was more important than this, and nothing has occurred in the more than two millennia since he lived to suggest otherwise. Death, and whatever may follow it, if anything, is still the great, seemingly unfathomable unknown, and the very thought of it continues to instill the deepest dread. And how much greater, then, the terror for someone actually facing an imminent descent into the void, the nothingness, of death. How can one possibly "prepare oneself" for the end of everything?

Plato, of course, gave us his dialogues to help enlighten us, and Evelyn Elsaesser, the author of this emotionally riveting book, following in this tradition, has now furnished us with what is effectively a kind of *monologue* on this same subject. But just as Plato's dialogues make for engrossing reading because of the liveliness of the interplay between Socrates and his interlocutors, so, too, has Evelyn hit on a literary device that compels from the start our deep engagement: she has written what appears to be a novel, or perhaps one might say more modestly "just a story", but in fact it is something else entirely. Just what it is and what it aims to accomplish is my task to explain in this introduction.

On the surface, *Talking with Angel* is the story of a young girl, told in the first person, who has contracted a serious disease. But don't be under any misconception, perhaps suggested by the title, that this is still another story of sentimental claptrap designed merely to tug at the reader's heartstrings. Or that it is a book about the supernatural intervention of angelic beings who bring inspirational messages of spiritual uplift and bland comfort. No, something else is going on here as we follow our unnamed heroine's journey during the course of her illness—a journey which, thanks to the author's literary skill and psychological insight, we also find ourselves taking with her.

Now, before going further, I need to note that of course it is not customary for a "novel" to require an introduction, and because this book has a novelistic form, it would be a disservice both to you and to the author if I were to divulge anything of the narrative line of the story that will unfold as soon as you start the book itself. However, because this book is not what it would at first blush appear to be, I can at least take a few liberties here to give you a sense of what this book is really about.

To begin with, we are in the mind of the narrator, the young girl, and from the outset, we are gripped by the drama of her illness. We enter her mind stream, her thoughts and feelings, as her illness develops. It is as if we become her diary—she is writing, she is confiding her innermost thoughts, to us. She draws us into her illness and its vicissitudes, and thus it is that we find ourselves sharing her journey and becoming intimately connected with her—and with the people in her life. Ultimately, her anguish becomes our own—but so, too, are the things she learns during the course of her struggle to understand and come to terms with what has happened to her. And these insights, the knowledge that comes to her, we come to see are the most important things. They are really what the book is about and what the book is designed to teach us.

The girl could be anyone—hence she is not given a name and we know very little about her, not even her age—but at the same time, there is something special about this girl. At the beginning of the story, she is seemingly quite ordinary, but as her illness progresses, so does she—in her knowledge, in the depth of her character, and, ultimately, in the profound degree of spiritual wisdom she attains as she confronts the possibility of "the end of everything". In short, this young girl goes through an accelerated course of personal and spiritual maturity so that by the time the book closes, she reminds us of someone like Anne Frank and we realize that we have been privileged to read another young girl's diary we will not soon forget.

During the course of our own journey through this book, we also come to appreciate that it is not a novel at all, notwithstanding its memoir-like form and the predominance of its interior monologue (although there is spoken dialogue as well). No, this is essentially a book of wisdom teachings — specifically, teachings about death and the possibility that something profound transcends death and can cast its light back on the living so as to transform them. And, just as with Plato's dialogues, so *Talking with Angel* is at bottom a mind-stretching philosophical undertaking dealing with one of the great perennial issues, but from a completely new contemporary perspective.

Much of Evelyn Elsaesser's life over the past decades has dealt with the phenomenon of the near-death experience, on which subject she is already recognized as an international authority. Her previous books and her many lectures have indeed gained for her a reputation as one of Europe's leading figures in this field. So, it is not surprising that it is the perspective of the near-death experience (or NDE, for short) that informs this book — and the life of her narrator (though in an unexpected way). But what Evelyn has done here is completely different from anything she has done before.

Her first book on the subject, *On the Other Side of Life*, was a scholarly and entirely academic treatment of the subject and consisted chiefly of interviews with various professionals in a number of diverse fields of specialization in which they commented learnedly on the NDE from the perspective of their particular disciplines. In her next book, *Lessons from the Light*, on which she collaborated with me, the focus was on what interested readers could learn from studies of the NDE so that they might be able to apply their implications to their own lives.

3

But in *Talking with Angel,* Evelyn departs completely from the world of the academy in order to tell a heartrendingly beautiful story that any person, even a child, could understand, relate to and learn from. Yet it is the special accomplishment of this book that everything essential about what the NDE teaches concerning what death is and about how life is meant to be lived from this understanding is conveyed so that any thoughtful reader can glean these insights and be transformed by them.

Which brings us finally to the questions of who this book is written for and how to make use of it. Clearly, from what I've already indicated, this is not "a children's book" or even one that is intended chiefly for teenagers or young adults—though readers from all of these groups could profit from it. Nor is it specifically intended for young persons who are ill or even facing death—though, again, such individuals are an obvious audience for a work of this kind. Similarly, one could highly recommend this book to parents of children suffering a serious illness since it provides such a vivid and compelling account of one young person's ordeal with the trauma of such a condition—and yet, once more, this category of reader is not necessarily the one that is most likely to benefit from reading the book.

I think you can see where I am heading with this. It's not that this book is meant for any one type of individual or for those in a special set of exigent circumstances. We are all death-bound, and we are all clinging to life; we are all in the same condition and we all will undergo the same fate. This book is for anyone who wants to break free of the cold grip of death. This is a book about liberation and how to attain it. Who could not be interested in it?

The book's method is not didactic, though there are teachings embedded in it. It is instead *experiential*. You learn from identification, through the natural power of empathy. The story will carry you: all you need to do is allow yourself to enter

4

into the narrator's frame of reference, and together you two will do the necessary work. The narrator is not a fictional person— she is you. Becoming her, you will find yourself—and your way home.

Kenneth Ring, Ph.D.
Professor Emeritus of Psychology, University of Connecticut (USA)

Part 1

1

"Where's Angel?"

"I don't know."

"I can't go without her; we've got to find her."

"All right," says Mum with a sigh, "I'll look for her, but then we must go."

It's three o'clock in the morning. I've been praying that it will be a false alarm, but my temperature is so high I have to accept that I shan't get away with it this time round. In spite of Mum's forced smile, I can tell she is worried stiff. And I am, too. You could say that this has become our normal state of mind, except you never get used to it. My little case is always ready, it only needs my sponge bag which Mum has just put in. I get dressed with difficulty. I feel weak, burning hot and in despair, but Mum doesn't give me any time to think about it. She gives me Angel who she found on my dressing table behind a pile of books, and we hurry out to the car. I sit on the back seat. Mum brings me a cushion and a thin blanket. When I have a high temperature, I go from intense sweating to violent shivering, and that is what is happening tonight. We don't even have time to take my temperature, but it must be more than 39 degrees. The car travels fast along the motorway. Usually Mum is a cautious driver, rather obsessive about speed limits, but when we go on these journeys to the hospital at night, she turns into a racing driver. I know that nothing will stop her getting me to the doctor as quickly as possible. It takes about one and a half hours to get to the hospital and I try to rest, because I know what is waiting for me there, but I can't sleep. I think over the year that has just gone by, and the beginning of the nightmare comes back into my mind.

~

It all started last year just before the summer holidays. I was really looking forward to them, because for several weeks we'd been getting ready for a trip to a Greek island called Zakynthos. A friend of Mum's had stayed there for several years. She had talked about it enthusiastically, describing such fabulous scenery that Mum had persuaded Dad to spend the whole month of July there. We had never gone away for such a long time. Dad wouldn't agree to it at the beginning because of his work, but Mum talked him round—and in the end he gave way, as he usually does. Mum showed me a brochure about the island. It was very beautiful, you could see little white houses, and the sea was a bright blue that merged into the sky along the horizon. I wanted to go there at once. Dad promised to hire surfboards and to teach me how to do it. I told him that it would be more likely to be me teaching him because we all know that he's not sporty and in fact quite clumsy. He had the grace to admit that this was probably what would happen. I was really excited at the thought that there were only three weeks of school left before we went.

Four days of school went by and I was tired and nervy without any apparent reason. On top of that my elbow hurt, but I couldn't remember having knocked it. I heard Mum telling Dad that evening when he came back from the office that I had been a nuisance and irritable all day. She didn't seem to be complaining about me, just stating a fact. I seem to have lost my appetite some time ago. My parents said that I ate like a sparrow. I thought this was a stupid expression, but it's true that my white jeans were too big, so I must have lost weight. The next day my right arm kept hurting off and on and I was so tired in the evening that I didn't make my usual protests to watch TV a bit longer. When Mum said, "Come on, love, it's bedtime," I sank on to the bed and fell asleep straightaway.

The next to last week of school was a real pain. Especially the Thursday because I quarrelled with Nicole, my best friend.

The argument started without any real reason. Nicole had quite simply got on my nerves. When I got home, I was crying, firstly because Nicole had gone off without trying to make it up, secondly because my arm still hurt, and finally because I was so tired that if anyone annoyed me in the least little bit, I felt tears come into my eyes. "You really do need a holiday, love," said Mum kindly. "Let's get this month over and set off for Greece." I was looking forward to it as well, but I kept wondering how I was going to manage to do surfing with my aching arm. What's more I had a very puzzling bruise on my thigh, and I came to the conclusion that I must have moved around and bumped myself in the night while I was asleep.

~

The week dragged on and I got no pleasure at all from going to school. My arm hurt all the time and so did my right knee. I just couldn't understand it, nothing like this had ever happened to me before. What's more the teacher had worried me by saying that I was dreadfully pale and that I looked as though I really needed a holiday. I made up the quarrel with Nicole, but got annoyed with David. To my great disappointment he seemed to have become as stupid as the other boys, and I told him so. "That's not true," he said, "I'm just the same as ever, it's you who's changed. You're always jumpy and in a bad temper." Who knows, perhaps he's right, I told myself in my heart of hearts without admitting it, of course. It was true I was irritable and I had had enough of having such an aching knee.

There was only the weekend and the following week to go. I knew that at school we would watch videos and play games because we never do any work the week before the summer holidays. That was lucky because I was finding it impossible to concentrate on what the teacher was explaining, especially in maths. In the whole of my life, I had never felt so tired. One morning I told Mum that my arm was hurting again. "Which arm?" she asked. "This one, my left arm," I replied. "Last time you were complaining that your arm ached, it was the right arm. We need to know..." She answered like this, rather dryly because she had enough of my "irritability" as she called it. For the past two weeks nothing had been the same, and I couldn't understand what was happening.

The next day was Sunday and I didn't wake up until midday. Mum let me sleep in, but she was worried when I finally appeared in the sitting room. It's true that normally at the weekend I'm the one who gets up first. "How do you feel?" asked Dad, "You look very pale."

"My ankle hurts," I replied. "Yesterday it was her left arm," Mum explained to Dad. "I think she's got growing pains. That would explain these pains in her bones, her tiredness and the paleness. What's more, she's eating so little I wonder if she has lost weight."

"Get on the bathroom scales tonight before you go to bed" she told me. "You'll have to buck up this time next week, you little imp," said Dad, "especially if you're meaning to teach me to surf..." A sudden wave of joy swept over me. It was true, we were off to Greece, to the sun, the sea and surfing. I wished I was there already.

~

Since the day before, I had been limping because my hip hurt. Mum was starting to get quite annoyed. She had never seen me like that before, edgy, tired and complaining first about one part of me and then another. The previous day we had gone shopping and Mum had bought me the most beautiful swimsuit that I'd ever seen. I decided to take it to school the next day to show to Nicole. While we were doing the shopping, I was very tired and I limped all the time. In the evening when we got back home, I'd stopped limping because it had stopped hurting. Mum commented in an irritated tone that either your leg hurt and you were limping, or it didn't hurt you and you weren't limping, but you had better make up your mind. She added that she didn't know what I was playing at. I didn't know either.

Two days later Mum made an appointment for me to see Dr Jordan, our family doctor. I thought she'd had enough of hearing me complain about my right knee, my left hand, my right arm, my left ankle... She admitted that I was indeed very pale, and she was a bit anxious because I'd lost two kilos. "Let's have a little check up like a car having a MOT," she said with a big smile. She was so pleased to be going to Zakynthos, and Dad was looking forward to it too.

Dr Jordan treated me kindly, as usual. I could see that Mum didn't really attach great importance to my little aches and pains, and above all she wanted the doctor to convince me that there was nothing wrong, that I was all right, so that I would stop complaining all the time. "It's true that she is pale," he added. "She really needs a holiday. I've always said that the timing of the school holidays is wrong. The summer term is too long from Easter to the end of June, they can't cope with it at that age. Enjoy yourself and have a rest unless you have something better to do," he said to me with a big smile. "Don't worry," he added turning to Mum, "it's true she does look tired, but I think she simply needs a holiday. If she's no better in a month when you come back from Greece, we'll do some tests, but for the moment I think it would be better to let her take full advantage of the holidays. I'm sure she'll come back fighting fit."

2

We arrived in Greece on a Saturday morning. The three weeks before we left had been very strange, almost frightening because I felt all sorts of unusual pains and had experienced states of mind which weren't like me at all. I was hoping to become myself again quickly and to forget these weeks of nervous irritation and confusion. The island of Zakynthos was really magnificent. Our hotel was very large, very beautiful. I had an enormous room all to myself with a balcony looking out over the sea, but in spite of all this, nothing was right. I felt so tired and weak that I refused to hire a surfboard, although Dad wanted to. What's more that morning I had a nosebleed which had never happened to me before. At the time I was a bit frightened, but the bleeding soon stopped. Mum suggested that I sat in the sun for a minute or two, she didn't like me looking so pale. In the evening my foot hurt so much that Dad had to support me when we went down to the hotel dining room. I wasn't hungry and I hardly ate anything even though the food looked delicious. My parents looked really worried and none of us felt as happy as we should have done considering the idyllic place we were in.

I spent the whole of Sunday lying stretched out under a sunshade. Dad had hired a surfboard and was making a show of enjoying himself trying to remain upright for more than a few seconds before falling into the water with a splash. I knew he was acting the clown in the hope that I would join him, to try to bring me out of this weird state which was so unlike me. My apathy wasn't intentional, but I was tired and sad, too tired and too sad to get up and run to Dad as I would have liked to. I was frightened, what was happening to me?

~

The next day Dad spent a long time on the phone talking to our travel agent and the airline with which we travelled to Greece. "It's an urgent matter," he repeated, "at all costs you must find three seats for us tonight, it's absolutely necessary." He spoke abruptly, his voice trembling with impatience, he who was normally so polite. But the flight was fully booked and so we were going to get the first plane next morning to go back home... Our holidays which were supposed to last a month were going to be over after only three days. I was lying down on my parents' bed, terrified, trying not to move in case it started again. I dared not turn my head suddenly, not take a deep breath in or out, nor even speak. That morning the most terrifying thing I had ever experienced had happened to me. I was brushing my teeth leaning over the washbasin when I felt something running down my nose. In a fraction of a second the basin was red all over. The blood which was running down my nostrils was mixing with the water coming from the tap and swirling away down the plughole. I was so scared that I stayed there petrified, my toothbrush in my hand. The blood was gushing from both my nostrils in strong regular spurts. I would never have guessed that my blood was so red. I turned off the tap, but that made it worse because it seemed to me that the washbasin was filling up with my blood which was no longer diluted nor carried away by the stream of water, and seemed to be gushing out faster than it could run away. I went into a complete panic and screamed "Mum, Dad, come here! I'm bleeding, I'm bleeding," but though their bedroom was next to mine, they couldn't hear me. I moved away from the basin to get a towel. That was when the blood ran on to the floor and on the pale yellow carpet where it left a red trail. I grabbed a white towel which I pressed very hard against my nose. I rushed into my parents' bedroom and took the towel away from my face to show them what was happening. I couldn't speak. Blood was running all over my lips, on my T-shirt and on the carpet. The stream of blood was still strong coming out of both nostrils at the same time, so I was breathing through my mouth. I could feel my heart pounding in my chest because I was so frightened. Mum had turned very pale because she had realized straight away what was happening to me. She ran into the bathroom. Dad was just looking at me. That's all he was doing, just looking. I could see surprise, incomprehension and panic come one after another into his eyes. Mum came back at once with a towel soaked in cold water which she put on the back of my neck. At the same time, she took my right hand and told me to pinch my nose with my thumb and first finger. "Press hard, harder," she ordered. The authority and the harsh tone of her voice made me realize how terrified she was too. I sat on their bed and released the pressure on my nose slightly. In a few seconds the blood was spreading all over my T-shirt which already had red spots on it, and all over my white shorts and my legs. I immediately pinched my nose again as hard as I could. It was then that I felt something running down my throat and I was swallowing a warm liquid. It was disgusting and I started to cough which made me take my hand away from my nose. Instantly there was blood everywhere all over me, the bed, everywhere. I was sobbing and gripping Mum's hand very hard, because I was so scared. She was trembling and mopped my brow with the wet towel she still had in her hands. The towel was red in some places, pink in others. I let go of my nose to try to breathe more than just through my mouth, because I felt I was suffocating. This was a mistake because the blood gushed out again, and ran on to my hand with even greater force. So, Mum pinched my nose hard, even violently. She put her other arm round me and pulled me towards her with a gesture so full of love and protection that it made tears come into my eyes. "Go down to the reception," she said to Dad. "Ask them for some *haemostatic* cotton wool."

"What sort of cotton wool?" stammered Dad. "Haemostatic!" shouted Mum, she who never raises her voice. Dad rushed out, and I leaned against Mum who pinched my nose very hard. I was breathing in gasps, through my mouth, terrified by all this blood and by this new thing which had come into my life so suddenly and unexpectedly. I knew by instinct that nothing would ever be the same again. Before this I had been carefree, I knew that from now on I would live in constant fear of it starting again, terrified of all this blood gushing out of my body, and by the certainty that death would be waiting for me when I had lost all my blood. I was still leaning against Mum who was pinching my nose very hard and I was swallowing the blood running down my throat. I could feel that Mum was tense and panic stricken, in spite of the comforting loving words she was whispering to me. I could imagine Dad at the reception asking for haemostatic cotton wool. "Yes, I said haemostatic, to stop the flow of blood. It's for my daughter who is bleeding and losing a great deal of blood..." How many litres of blood do we have in our bodies? I told myself that if it didn't stop, I would die. But how could it stop since I was bleeding more and more? I gripped Mum's hand so hard that it hurt me. I couldn't manage to speak because I was swallowing all the time... and Dad hadn't yet come back. I felt very weak and at the same time, strange to say, I felt so good leaning against Mum. I had the impression that I was gently sliding towards the night. There was a black frame around my field of vision and I felt a deep peace and a great desire to close my eyes, to abandon myself to this attractive velvety dark. I was about to faint. If I could have died at that moment in my state of distress and at the same time in the great wellbeing which Mum's presence created, I think I would have agreed, but Dad came back with the haemostatic cotton wool, and life began again with its panic. "She has been bleeding for a long time," Mum said, her voice shaking, as she let go of my nose. I immediately took over and pinched it hard. My parents asked me to let go of my nose because they wanted to insert the cotton wool into it. I was too frightened at the thought

17

of seeing streams of blood again, so I refused. So, they held my hand by force and put pieces of cotton wool into my nostrils. I was exhausted and the black edges closed in around my field of vision once again. I felt so weak that I wanted to close my eyes again. I was a prey to an unknown fatigue, a sort of resignation, as if I were abandoning this life. The call was at the same time gentle, tempting, and terribly dangerous. The pieces of cotton wool pushed into my nostrils had stopped the haemorrhage. I dared neither move nor speak. I couldn't bear the thought of the bleeding starting again. I had never needed Mum so much, never been so frightened, had never felt so close to death, and that feeling would never go away. In one hour, I had become aware of the fragility of life, of the fact that blood could escape from my body and that I could die. I had also realized that my parents who I had previously looked on as very strong people who knew everything and who had complete power over me, and perhaps even over the whole world, even they could do nothing about my blood which was coming out of my body, spreading everywhere and making me so afraid, and which could cause my death.

Several hours had passed since the bleeding stopped. I had refused to let them take out the haemostatic cotton wool that was blocking my nostrils. I was still breathing through my mouth and felt as if I were suffocating. My lips were dry and I was terribly thirsty. From time to time I swallowed clots of blood. It was disgusting, but I was so afraid of causing the bleeding to start again that I didn't dare clear my throat, or speak, or get up, or take out the cotton wool, and I certainly didn't have the courage to blow my nose. I knew my life had taken a new turn that day on the island of Zakynthos, a decisive turn from which there was no going back. I knew fear, panic-stricken fear, the fear of dying.

~

"It's hot, Dad," I said in the airport lounge where we were waiting for them to announce our flight. "You'll feel better in the plane," replied Dad. "It's air-conditioned." But it was even worse in the plane. I was sweating and my hair was damp. Dad put his hand on my forehead and I could feel his fingers go tense. "You've got a temperature, my darling," he said in a rather strangled voice. "You're burning hot." I sat in a window seat but for the first time on a plane, I closed my eyes. I usually loved watching the scenery go by below me, or admiring the fluffy clouds which made me want to jump on them and bounce. This time I felt too ill, I didn't want to see anything.

I had been very frightened in Greece, but I didn't realize that this was nothing compared to what was waiting for me back home.

3

From the airport we went straight to Dr Jordan's surgery. Dad had let him know we'd arrived, and he was waiting for us. It was Tuesday midday; our holiday had been very short.

The way the doctor looked at me made me alarmed. He was worried, you could see that. This time it was no longer a question of the summer term being too long, and the need for rest in the absence of more exciting things to do. The doctor spoke of the necessity of thorough medical tests, and a full examination to discover the cause of my symptoms. He thought it might be glandular fever. "They'll take good care of you in the hospital, you'll see, everybody's very kind there," he said with an attempt at a reassuring smile. "Better go straightaway."

"Without even going home first?" asked Mum, who seemed more upset by the urgency the doctor's advice implied than by the inconvenience that it would cause. "I think that would be best," replied the doctor calmly.

The holidays were finished, and perhaps my days of happiness too. Sometimes you understand something even if you don't know it yet. I felt a certainty that was both confused and yet clear. It was quite scary.

The hospital was a long way away and very large. "It's the university hospital," said Dad, as if that would console me. We got there after what seemed to me to be an endless journey. Dr Jordan had told them we were coming. So as soon as we arrived, a nurse took me into an ugly room where she weighed and measured me and put me into a bed with rough sheets. Then she gave me a thermometer. I had a temperature of over 39 degrees. This didn't surprise me, I really felt very hot. A bit later a young doctor came in and started to examine me very thoroughly, my stomach, my heart, and my lungs in order to do a complete assessment as he called it. Then there came another nurse who took me into a big room with two chairs with funny armrests. She sat me in one of them, smiled at me and said, "My name is Agnes. I'm a champion with the needle, so the other children tell me, therefore there isn't much chance of it hurting when I take blood—or give you an injection." I could see she was trying to put me at ease, but I had just spent a very distressing morning and the best I could manage was a forced smile. Agnes inspected the veins on the inside of my elbows and settled for the right arm. She tapped it to make the vein stand out, and tightened a rubber band around my arm. Five tubes with different coloured lids were placed in a little tray beside me, along with some antiseptic, some balls of cotton wool, a dressing and a syringe, which was still wrapped up. On shelves which ran the length of the wall there stood small tubes with lids of at least twenty different shades of colour. On the upper shelves there were extra tubes also arranged according to colour, immediately above the same tubes which had been unwrapped. I told myself that they must take blood from lots of people day after day to need so many tubes, but in fact I couldn't have cared less. I was just trying to occupy my mind, because I don't like having blood taken. "Watch out, the needle is going in," said Agnes in a joyful tone of voice which didn't seem to me to be suited to the occasion. It is true that I hardly felt anything when the needle went into my vein. She took out a large quantity of blood. This time the sight of my blood didn't frighten me, perhaps because Agnes was in control, only taking as much as was needed. Once the needle was taken out, the blood stopped flowing and that reassured me.

Back in my room I was relieved to be put into a bed, even if it wasn't my own. I fell asleep almost at once, and was wakened by the whispering of the young doctor who was explaining to my parents the first results of the blood tests. I was too tired to open my eyes, so they all thought I was asleep. "I won't hide from you that I'm worried about the number of white blood cells," he said, "more than 80,000, that's unusually high. I've asked for a second blood test because I thought there might be some mistake."

"And what does this high number of white cells mean, doctor?" asked Dad in a voice that didn't sound like his. "A serious infection, I suppose?"

"Yes, but as yet we don't know the cause of it. For the moment I'm just going to prescribe paracetamol for her to reduce the fever. When we've found out the cause of the infection, we'll adjust the treatment. I've contacted Professor Granger who will come as soon as we have all the results available." I went back to sleep, happy to know that my parents were at my side.

~

I spent the afternoon half asleep. As soon as I was completely awake, Mum gave me a drink. The nightmare really started with the arrival of Professor Granger. He was quite old and looked very kind. He had lots of wrinkles round his eyes, and he smiled all the time, but even so his face looked sad. He sat on my bed, patted my hand, looked at my parents one after another, seemed almost about to say something, but then didn't speak. We stayed like this for a long time in silence. Outside it was still daylight and I could hear children shouting in the distance. Then the Professor cleared his throat and said in a hesitant voice, "We now have the results of the blood tests. I'm sorry to tell you that they aren't good. You are very ill," he said to me, looking straight into my eyes as if offering me something to hang on to, and conveying to me his sadness, his compassion, and also his strength. "Your blood count has shown pathological cells. White corpuscles are reproducing in your blood in excessive quantities. Instead of growing and maturing they are multiplying in a wild and uncontrolled manner, while still remaining in an immature state. They don't play their part in fighting off infection, that is

22

why you have such a high temperature. What is more, you are short of red blood cells and you are tired because it is the red corpuscles which transport oxygen. Your illness is also bringing about a shortage of blood platelets, and this can cause bleeding which isn't always easy to stop."

He stopped talking and waited patiently for his words to sink into our minds, but nobody seemed to understand, neither my parents nor myself. There was a long silence. You could feel the fear hovering around the room, the fear of asking, the fear of understanding. The professor took my hand which he squeezed. I could feel his warmth. Time seemed to have stopped and I was so tense that my head was spinning. I knew instinctively that the next words to be spoken would seal my fate. As long as no one spoke, nothing would be understood and nothing would be real. But time doesn't ever let itself be suspended for long, it is as cruel and pitiless as truth. My father came out of his stupor and asked in a trembling voice, "It's not really serious, I suppose? It can surely be treated? With antibiotics anything can be cured these days, can't it?"

"In actual fact it can be treated," replied Professor Granger patiently, "chemotherapy is becoming more and more effective." At this moment Mum gave a frightened little cry like a baby bird which sounded so ridiculous that at any normal time I would have burst out laughing. She sometimes does make strange noises and she is the first to smile about them. Even if I didn't understand what in the doctor's words had upset her so much, I realized that our carefree times had gone forever. All this was too much for me. I had the impression of being here and elsewhere at the same time. When I'm very tired or completely thrown by events, I have this feeling of not knowing where I am any more. Everything becomes unreal, I no longer know if I'm living in the present, or if it is all happening in my imagination, in a dream perhaps, in a nightmare certainly! I fell back on to the pillow, closed my eyes and turned to face the wall. I didn't want to hear any more, and certainly not to understand! "Let's give her a little rest now," whispered the doctor to my parents. "Please come with me into the corridor, I have a few more details to discuss with you." All three went out of my room and I remained facing the wall, unable to breathe normally, panicking, exhausted and at the same time curiously indifferent, as if none of this concerned me. I tried to sleep. My temperature had risen again. I was burning hot, and I had a headache.

~

I must have fallen asleep for a moment, because my parents woke me when they came back into the room. At first, I hardly recognized them. It seems ridiculous, of course, who couldn't recognize their own parents? And yet it is true, they weren't the same as before. They were very pale, as if physically stunned, but this was only their outward appearance. The real change was inside them and you could see it in their eyes—the way they looked was so full of anguish that my heart turned to stone. "What's happening?" I muttered. "What's wrong with me?" Dad sat down so close to me that he sat on my arm. "I'm sorry," he said, moving away a bit. He leaned towards me and put his arm round me. His need to touch me was in proportion to his fear of talking to me. For a long time, he remained without saying anything, holding me very tightly, and rather clumsily. In fact, he was suffocating me a bit, but I didn't say anything. That day everything was going wrong in all sorts of ways. After a long time, I gently disentangled myself and sat up. I wanted to go to sleep, but before I did, I was anxious for them to tell me a little bit more. This sudden dangerous need to know was probably due to the fact that I wanted to get it over with. It was at this moment that Dad burst into sobs. The last time I had seen him cry was at the cemetery when my grandma had died. His sobs were violent, uncontrolled, full of despair. He turned away and looked for something in his trouser pocket. A hanky no doubt, but I knew that he never had one on him. He himself must have known this, I suppose. Mum passed him a paper tissue. She was crying too. But what's happening? I wondered. Okay, I have a high temperature and too many white blood cells, as they say, but that can be treated, the doctor had said so. Mum came to sit on the other side of the bed, she took my arm and kissed the palm of my hand like she used to do when I was little. "You've got leukaemia, my love," she said in a toneless voice. I had already heard this word, but I didn't really know what it meant. My parents' reaction made me realize how serious it was. It was in their eyes that I saw the extent of the catastrophe. I didn't have the strength or the desire to ask for further details. We stayed for a long time in a silence that isolated us from one another the longer it lasted. Unhappiness separates people, that is true. Joy can be shared, but not suffering. Night was falling slowly, tinting the sky a magnificent red colour. How I would have liked to be back on the island of Zakynthos! It was still only Tuesday of the first week of the summer holidays, and all this was surely a nightmare. This feeling of unreality came over me again. I wasn't myself. The one positive thing about nightmares is that you get an immense feeling of relief when they are over. When would I wake up?

4

I must have nodded off again. This time it was Professor Granger who woke me. My parents were still there, Dad sitting at the end of my bed, Mum in an armchair at the back of the room. It was almost completely dark apart from a pale light which still faintly lit up the horizon. "I've arranged for the bone marrow sample to be taken at nine o'clock tomorrow morning," he said. He looked tired too. "That will help us to know the extent of the illness, and above all which treatment to apply." When the doctor said the words "bone marrow sample" I saw my parents shudder. I wanted to know how they would perform the bone marrow sample and the doctor explained it at length. The panic rising in me prevented me from understanding, nonetheless I grasped the idea that the doctor was going to take a small quantity of liquid from my bone to analyse it. "Bone marrow is a soft substance found in bones," he told me. I asked if he was going to stick something into the inside of my arm to take out the bone marrow, like the nurse had done in the morning to take a blood sample. "No," he replied. "Well then, are you going to prick my finger, because I've got bones in my fingers?" He smiled kindly, then he said, "No, that would not do. We are going to take the liquid from the pelvic bone. You will not feel anything because we'll give you something to send you to sleep." Now I understood why Dad and Mum looked so terrified when the doctor had spoken of "bone marrow sample." They were worried because they knew I would have to have a general anaesthetic.

My parents had gone home after promising to come back early next morning to be with me at the time of the bone marrow sample. I would have liked them to stay with me all night, but I kept quiet, telling myself that after all I wasn't a baby, although... that evening I felt very small and frightened. It seemed to me that since going to Greece, fear had never left me. Before that, I wasn't afraid of anything except spiders and sometimes an oral exam, but you can't really call that fear, rather more like a funk.

~

At dawn I still had a high temperature which was being brought down by the medicine that I had to take every four hours. As I was less tired than the day before, I had more awareness of reality and it was agonizing. I had grasped that I had leukaemia, but I couldn't understand all the implications. Mum and Dad rushed in about nine o'clock. The hospital is a long way from our house. They brought me a little case with some things in it. Mum had also thought of bringing me Angel. Angel is my favourite doll. I know that I'm too old to play with dolls, but this one is very special, because she was knitted by my grandma whom I loved very much. Since she died, Angel has become my favourite since she's all I have left of Grandma, except for my memories, of course.

"Dad and I had a talk yesterday evening," said Mum, sitting on the edge of my bed. "Of course, you aren't just suffering from a simple cold but an illness which is more serious, but there's nothing to panic about. Leukaemia can be treated very well nowadays. Dad called his friend Andrew yesterday, you know, the one who's a doctor. He totally agreed with Professor Granger's comments. The path to recovery won't be simple, you'll need a lot of patience, but we will be on your side and everything will be all right."

"Together we'll defeat your illness much quicker than you imagine, you'll see!" added Dad with a big smile. I turned towards them and gave a deep sigh. I felt much better and could finally relax. I smiled back at them. They were right, everything would turn out fine in the end.

The nurse called Agnes had come to fetch me, and we were all waiting for Professor Granger in a little white impersonal

27

room. He arrived with a big smile and told me that he was going to remove a little bit of liquid from the marrow of my ilium. "I bet you don't know where your ilium is?" he said to tease me. "No, I don't know," I replied. "It's there," he said, pointing to the top of my pelvis. Then everybody became very professional, and nobody made any more jokes, certainly not me. Mum held my hand. Professor Granger explained that they were going to ask me to breathe into a mask which would send me to sleep while they went ahead with the bone marrow sample. The idea that I was going to be unconscious and entirely at their mercy made me panic. I felt completely stressed out, and my heart was pounding away in my chest. What was happening to me was quite different from taking a blood sample, was nothing like that at all. It was a thousand times worse. "Try to relax," advised the doctor, but there was no question of doing that, I was in far too much of a panic. I was breathing through my mouth jerkily, and that was making my head spin. Then they put on the mask and I lost consciousness almost immediately. When I woke up, Professor Granger told me it had all gone well, and Agnes who was gently stroking my hair added, "It's all over. You were very brave, a model patient. I think we're going to keep you in our hospital!" This was the first time that I had gone through such a frightening examination, but it was also my first contact with the very special humour of the carers. The words they say aren't always particularly funny, but that isn't the important thing. What counts is their desire to make us sick children laugh, to distract us from our distress and our pain, their determination to comfort us any way they can.

At about five o'clock another nurse called Denise took me for the X-rays. "Why are they doing this?" I asked. "To see if everything's okay," she replied. That's stupid, I thought, they know everything's *not* okay, rather that *nothing's* okay since I've got leukaemia. The radiology assistant asked me to turn in different positions and she took several X-rays. The contact with the hard, cold plate of the X-ray machine made me shiver every time, and I began to feel that I'd really had enough. Back in my room, Denise took my temperature. Like the evening before it had gone up again, and I had another headache. The nurse brought me a paracetamol and some herb tea. I felt completely stunned, as if someone had hit me on the head. By that I mean that everything was so different, so worrying, that I no longer felt like the same person.

~

That night I woke up with a sweat at two o'clock in the morning. I switched on the light, knowing that I was alone in the room without my parents. I felt terribly abandoned and I started to cry. The more I cried the more wretched I felt and I cried all the more, to such an extent that I started to choke. I tried to calm myself but nothing worked. All this was too much for me, I couldn't cope. What was this nightmare that had already lasted too long? In my panic I pressed the bell above my bed. I wanted to talk to someone. I couldn't bear being alone any longer. Soon afterwards the door opened and a cheerful face appeared. "What's the matter?" asked a nurse. "Aren't you asleep?"

"No," I answered sobbing, "I'm afraid." She came to me and took my hand. "My name's Sarah," she said, "and I'm here to look after girls like you who are afraid in the night." She stayed for some time, stroking my hair and talking to me gently about all sorts of unimportant things. Then she took my temperature and decided to give me some more medicine. I found that I was taking a lot of it these last few days, and I hate doing that. Sarah had to continue her round, but she promised to come back later. When I awoke again, it was morning.

My parents came back at about eight o'clock. I was sitting up in bed drinking a cup of chocolate. I couldn't manage to eat anything. Denise came in to tell me that the morning schedule included an MRI scan and taking some more blood samples as well as my temperature and blood pressure. I had experienced nicer mornings in my life! I didn't know what an MRI scan was and Dad explained to me that it was a machine which worked on magnetic resonance. I couldn't understand his explanation, but as I didn't really want to know, I didn't insist and decided to let it be a surprise. It was a nasty surprise because I discovered that I was going to be put into a very narrow tube. I had to lie down on a sort of stretcher which was then slid into a tunnel. It was so tiny that I could almost touch the sides. Only my head was in a less restricted space. A mirror fixed just above my eyes allowed me to see the room behind my head. In addition to this, by means of a microphone, I could communicate with the technician who was sitting behind a computer in an adjacent room. I felt as though I couldn't breathe. I was alone in the room and the examination took a long time. The noise of the machine was loud and irritating, and I was all on edge. The technician had told me I could talk to her at any time though the microphone if I had a problem. Suddenly, I felt I couldn't stand any longer being in such an uncomfortable position, lying on my back, and the horrible feeling that I couldn't move with this tunnel round my body. The thought of a coffin came to my mind and frightened me.

"I want to get out!" I cried in panic. "It's not possible just now," she answered, "I'm asking you to be patient a bit longer, the examination is nearly over."

"It's me, Mum," came Mum's voice over the loudspeaker. "We're here with you in the room next door. Don't worry, everything's all right." That's going a bit far, I thought, I'd rather say everything has been wrong for some days now. But I understood that calling out and complaining wouldn't shorten the examination, and so I decided to put up with it patiently. Finally, I was taken out of the horrible machine and allowed to go back to my room. I was already thinking of this ugly room as "mine" though I wasn't intending to stay there for very long.

5

At about four in the afternoon Professor Granger came back, holding some files under his arm. My parents and I had been waiting for quite a long time. That was the new lesson I had learnt: in hospital you have one main occupation—waiting! It is exhausting, contrary to what you might think. What's more, it's worrying, because you never know what bad news is about to break.

He sat on my bed and patted my hand. "How are you?" he asked. It was a question that I was going to hear often in the months to come. "I'm okay," I said, thinking the opposite. "We've got all the results now," he went on. "First of all, I'm going to explain the illness to you, the treatments we are considering, and then you can ask me all the questions you want. So, as I told you, we are dealing with a case of leukaemia, more precisely acute lymphoblastic leukaemia or A.L.L. As you know, it's a disease of the blood that causes an uncontrolled proliferation of the white corpuscles. I've already described the broad lines of the illness the other day. You will remember that we found a very high number of white blood corpuscles in the first blood count, more than 80,000. Today I want to talk to you about the treatment that we're going to start without delay. Leukaemia can be treated very effectively nowadays. People think immediately of a fatal outcome when talking about acute leukaemia in a child, but this belongs fortunately to the past. Chemotherapy has become very effective these days."

"Chemotherapy," said Mum looking upset, "is it really necessary?"

"Yes," replied the doctor, who was obviously used to dealing with this sort of question. "It is indispensable since it's the only remedy we have available at present. The initial treatment enables us to obtain a complete remission, that's to say, a return to the normal clinical haematological state. The subsequent treatment is intended to eliminate the residual leukaemia cells which could perhaps cause a relapse."

As I didn't understand what chemotherapy was, I couldn't understand why Mum was so upset. "Is it tablets or injections?" I asked on the off chance. "It is a liquid which is introduced into your body intravenously," explained the doctor, smiling kindly at me. "You see, we must at all costs eliminate these malign cells. To neutralize them, we must destroy them. That is the purpose of the chemotherapy: to kill the diseased cells in order to cure you. You'll have a whole series of chemotherapies to go through in succession, spread out in time. In between you can go home, go to school if you feel like it, and lead an almost normal life. You will come back to see me quite regularly so that I can control the state of your blood. I don't want to hide from you that this route will be difficult, full of setbacks, and that you will have to be very brave and patient. There will be times when you don't want to see me again, to have tests done and to wait for results. But this is the price of the cure and you will have to draw up a new philosophy of life."

I saw tears running down Mum's face. I looked at Dad and realized that he was clenching his teeth so hard that you could see the outline of his cheek muscles. He often did this when he was nervous and Mum and I used to tell him that it was bad for him. I still didn't understand really what they were talking about. All right, I had leukaemia, they were going to introduce a liquid into my body intravenously and I would often have to come back to the hospital. But I couldn't really see the consequences that all this was going to have on my life.

"What's your prognosis?" asked Dad. You could see that he either wanted an encouraging reply or none at all. "I can't say at the moment," replied the doctor. "It will depend in part on your daughter's response to the induction treatment. But I can at this point give you some reassuring news: the tests haven't revealed any tumour. So, we will not be fighting on two fronts." I understood what he had just said meant that I didn't have cancer. "I'm pleased that I haven't got cancer," I said, greatly relieved. At last, I felt better for the first time in days. My energy immediately came back, and I felt a sort of explosion of joy, probably due to the huge relief that came over me. I knew this nightmare would end one day. I had remained convinced that nothing really terrible could happen to me. I was ill, okay, but it wasn't really very, very serious, since I hadn't got cancer. "You have what is sometimes called cancer of the bone marrow," said the doctor, with a look of great sadness in his eyes. I could see that he hated to give me this bad news. This time I really understood what a great catastrophe it was. I had got cancer; I hadn't understood this before. It is difficult to describe what happened to me at that moment. It was like a huge wave breaking over me and sweeping me off the ground. I was in the grip of such a powerful vertigo that I lost all sense of up and down. At the same time, I felt as if someone had punched me violently in the stomach. I gave a scream which made me jump and come out of this spaced-out state in which I found myself. At the same time, I felt I was suffocating, and that made my head dizzy. I think I lost consciousness for a short while. I didn't want to know any more. When was I going to wake up from this nightmare? It couldn't be true. I had *not* got cancer. It wasn't possible. I thought about a book that I'd read the previous year in the library at school. It was a story about a little boy who died of cancer and it was really too sad. I had kept back my tears, because I didn't want Nicole, who was sitting reading beside me, to see me crying. And now this man, sitting on my bed in this ugly room, was telling me that I had cancer. It was unreal; I shut my eyes and turned towards the wall. "Let her have a little rest," said the doctor, "I will come back at the end of the afternoon to carry on with our discussion."

I didn't want to talk, and I kept my eyes shut to indicate to my parents that it wasn't even worthwhile trying. I felt completely gutted, dumbfounded and thoughts refused to form in my mind. It was quite simply a total void, and that was the only thing that I could bear at that moment.

I kept dozing off, forgetting this catastrophe which had struck me, but each time I emerged from my sleepiness, I was overcome with the oppressive feeling that something terrible had happened, and the memory struck me forcibly: I had cancer! The same panic seized me all over again. It was true, I had forgotten... I had cancer! I sobbed and buried my head in the pillow. Dad and Mum stroked me in silence, and I went back to sleep. The afternoon went by like this, the attempts to forget by going to sleep alternating with violent shocks due to remembering what had become a reality: *I had cancer.*

6

In the evening Professor Granger came back, but I didn't want to see him. He was the person through whom this disaster had come into my life, at least he was the messenger. The discussion took place between him and my parents. I turned my back on them, facing the wall, but I could hear what they were saying. The chemotherapy was going to start in two days' time. The next day I was going to be rehydrated. The doctor said that no time must be wasted before starting the treatment. The induction chemotherapy, the "attack" as he called it, would probably last four weeks, depending on my response to the initial treatment, at the rate of five or ten minutes a session. The secondary effects were well known and were quite easy to overcome: nausea (although there were very effective medicines to treat it) and great tiredness. Then the main risk was infection due to the breaking down of the immune system. "It is several days after the end of the chemotherapy that the risk of infection is greatest, because the initial treatment is tough so as to give us a good chance of success," added the doctor. "To give *me* a good chance, he means," I said to myself. "He hasn't got cancer as far as I know!" I felt very much alone, excluded from the world of healthy people. From that moment, this feeling would haunt me, this cruel impression of being different, isolated, alone in my unhappiness and with my anguish.

Professor Granger gave us lots of details about the treatment, but I was no longer listening to him. I started to pay attention again when he spoke of the coming months, and of what my illness would mean to our family life and to my future at school. "I shall give up my job," said Mum. "Wait a while before taking this decision, perhaps it won't be necessary," the doctor advised. "And what about school?" asked Dad. "Usually that doesn't cause too many problems," replied the doctor. "For your daughter the timing is quite fortunate, because we are at the beginning of July. There's no doubt she will be ready to go back to school in September. Children who are ill have this in common, they want to go back to school as quickly as possible. They are brave and persistent. They often only follow the main part of the curriculum and stop studying the secondary subjects, which allows more time for rest. School becomes very important to them, because it symbolizes a goal in life. They are often excellent students even if they miss lessons more often than their friends. To compensate they concentrate and apply themselves more than others. Incidentally you will discover the solidarity and friendship that young people are capable of when one of them is in difficulties—it really teaches us what life is about! All this is of prime importance for the patient, and contributes greatly towards the cure. Illness is an ordeal, no doubt about that, but the affliction can make people grow. It often enriches the person who is ill, and those around them, in a spectacular way," he added with a touch of gentleness. I wasn't with him; I was still trying to swallow the bitter pill: my sentence had been pronounced: I had cancer!

~

We hardly spoke anymore that evening. The stress of the last few days had exhausted us. Mum was very pale. My parents had gone home. I switched on the television which had just been put in my room. Dad had asked for it to be done. The pictures flickered before my eyes without any sense. I kept changing channels, there were 32 of them. My eyes were burning and I had a bad headache. Then I decided to switch off the TV but that made it worse, because the thoughts came flooding in, and I was submerged by anguish as if by a tidal wave. So, I switched it back on again and for some time stayed watching the succession of pictures and hearing sounds that were meaningless to me. At that moment Sarah came into my room. She was young and very pretty. I hadn't realized this the night before. I was pleased she was on duty and I asked if we could talk for a while. "Okay," she replied, "until somebody calls me to another room, or until my next round starts. What's your day been like?" she asked briskly, sitting down on my bed. "Awful," I replied, "I've got cancer."

"I know," she said.

"Well, I didn't know, and what's more I still can't believe it," I said. "That's normal," she reassured me. "This type of bad news is a terrible shock, and it takes time to deal with it. But tell yourself that leukaemia can be treated easily these days, unlike twenty years ago. You were born at the right time, my pet," she added laughing.

"You're actually telling me that I'm lucky!" I said, feeling offended. "I wouldn't go so far as to say that, that would be an exaggeration," she admitted. "You're not the only person on this floor to have leukaemia. At the moment we have eleven children and teenagers with different kinds of cancer. Did you know that?" I hadn't realized that there were other young people, and I was pleased not to be the only child in this hospital. And what's more they had cancer too. I immediately felt not quite so alone. "I'd like to see them," I said. "Tomorrow you'll be able to meet them, at least most of them. You will find them in the common room or in the dining room at meal times," said Sarah.

"Why won't I be able to see all of them?" I asked.

"Because three of them are in isolation, they are waiting for a transplant."

"A transplant of what?" I asked. "Of bone marrow," replied Sarah, without giving any more details. I didn't want to know any more for the moment. I felt there would be ample opportunity for that later. Sarah had understood, of that I was sure. "Good, I'm going," she said cheerfully as she stood up. "Try to go to sleep a bit. But if you can't, you may call me, but switch off this stupid TV. At this time of night there's nothing worth watching in any case." It was past midnight and this time I managed to go to sleep. I was pleased to know I wasn't the only sick child in this hospital.

7

The next day I was woken up at seven. I wanted to sleep longer, but I wasn't given the chance. Denise took my temperature and my blood pressure, and brought me my hot chocolate. She also brought the rest of the breakfast, wagging her finger at me playfully: "Today you must eat, my pet. While you are having chemo you won't be very hungry, so you must make good use of the one day left." I obeyed and ate everything. I even drank the orange juice which I don't really like much. I felt a bit less desperate than the day before. The thought of the presence of other children was doing me good even if I didn't know them yet. It wasn't long before I met them. As soon as I saw them, I felt my legs give way: they looked scary, pale, ill, and the most horrible thing, some of them had no hair! I was overcome with a feeling of revulsion, and at the same time I felt sorry for them. How ill they must have been to have lost their hair! They looked like walking corpses with their bald heads, their pale faces, and their huge eyes set deep in their sockets. I who had been so delighted to meet them was now running away from them. In fact, I went out of the common room as quickly as politeness allowed. I ran back to my room and threw myself on to the bed and burst into sobs. "This is obviously not a holiday camp," I told myself reproachfully. "What did you expect? You're in a hospital, and in a hospital, there are sick people. And *you* are one of them," I told myself suddenly with horror, with a sudden flash of realization. "I'm ill too, just like them. Only with me it can't be seen." Denise came in at this moment. She had seen me running past the nurses' room and she came to comfort me. "What's the matter?" she asked gently. "What's frightened you so much?"

"The children," I said, wiping my eyes. "They're so horrible to look at, especially the ones with no hair."

"Ah yes, but why horrible?" she asked, pretending to be astonished. "They look as though they're dead," I answered. "Not at all," she replied, laughing. "Do you think a few strands of hair make the difference between the living and the dead?" "No, of course not," I had to admit. "But I'm terrified of them. You can see all the bumps on their skulls and their big ears stuck on like cabbage leaves."

"Okay," she said, "and what else?"

"And their great big eyes which are so intense that they're scary," I added. "And what's more, they look very ill, exhausted, and they are white like corpses."

"All that is true," agreed Denise with a reassuring smile. "It's true, but none of that can justify your fear. You are simply not used to seeing children with no hair, that's all. Their tiredness is due to their treatment, but it will pass. They are pale, that's true too, but wait until we have taken good care of them for a while, you'll see the nice pink colour that comes back to their skin! In a few days you won't take any notice of that, you'll see. Don't just go by their appearance. You know that hair grows again, and more quickly than you would think." I felt better, she was right. However, there remained in my head the outline of a question which I couldn't put into words. But I didn't want to express it clearly, something inside me refused to do it. "You are right," I said to Denise with a smile, "Perhaps I'll go back to them."

"Not now," replied Denise kindly. "We're going to put in the little reservoir."

"The what?"

"The reservoir," she said laughing. "You know, for the injections and the blood samples! Didn't Professor Granger explain that to you yesterday?"

"He might, I wasn't listening," I admitted.

"Ah well, I see!" she said teasingly. "Okay, I will tell you again, but only if you listen. We are putting in a little box about the size of a two pence piece under your skin, level with your chest. This box will be connected to a central vein, and each time we need to take a blood sample or give you some medicine, we can inject it into this little box. It will be used to hydrate you today, and also to inject your chemo treatment from tomorrow onwards. What's more, it'll allow us to give you a medicine very quickly, if you need it for some reason or another. You see it's practical, it's multifunctional."

"Anyone would think you're trying to sell me something," I replied. My remark made her burst out laughing. "I like it when you make jokes, my pet. It does me good to hear you teasing me." The nurses certainly laughed a lot in this hospital and that did me good too.

An hour later, I was equipped with the famous box which I had taken good care not to look at when it was placed on a little tray. I preferred not to know what I was going to carry around in my chest. To put it in required a general anaesthetic, and as with the first one, I went into a panic because I felt so out of control. Agnes, who was back after a day off, put me into bed and attached me to a drip by means of this famous box. "What is it?" I asked, looking at the transparent liquid flowing in a thin stream into my veins from the plastic bag via a tube. "It's a rehydrating solution made up of sugar, salt and water," Agnes explained. "That's to get you ready for the chemo tomorrow, so that you'll be fit." I really found their remarks very optimistic!

~

The next day shortly before eleven Denise came to give me my first dose of chemo. At first, I felt nothing, but a slight queasiness quickly spread all over me. I couldn't really describe what this feeling was like, it was perhaps simply due to my nervousness. Denise noticed this and explained again the purpose of the chemo. "You see, we've got to get rid of these bad cells. The white corpuscles form in the bone marrow. When someone has leukaemia, these cells don't grow normally. They remain immature and become uncontrollable, multiplying in an anarchic manner. The medicine which is carefully calculated and which I'm injecting into you will kill these cancerous cells. Unfortunately, at the same time it will neutralize some of the healthy cells. This is the price of the cure, as you might say. The destruction of healthy cells will make you tired, will exhaust you on occasions, so you will need a lot of rest. As Professor Granger explained to you, you'll have to take care to keep away from infection as much as possible. Your natural defences, which are also called your immune system, will be weakened after the chemotherapy. It's mainly for this reason that you will stay here for several weeks. During this time your system will need a bit of fine-tuning. Then it will get on all right by itself again. We will also keep an eye on the fluidity of your blood. If it is too liquid, it can cause haemorrhages."

"Blood that's too liquid, can that cause nose bleeding?" I asked in alarm.

"Yes, exactly, but why do you ask that?" the nurse inquired.

"Because my nose bled so much in Greece, I thought all my blood would empty out of me," I explained.

"Yes, I read that in your notes," replied Denise. "This sort of bleeding often occurs in cases of leukaemia."

"Can it happen again?" I asked in terror.

"We'll do all we can to avoid it," Denise reassured me and patted my hand. "Don't worry, if it should happen, we'd always be able to stop the bleeding, even if it sometimes takes a little longer than we would like. That's finished," she said, taking out the drip. "How do you feel?"

"I'm all right," I replied without conviction. I still felt a bit strange. Some hours later when the setting sun coloured the sky an intense shade of red, I knew exactly how I felt: ill!

I was sick all night. Sarah was not on duty, and I was sorry about that. The night nurse was called Madge, she wasn't so nice. Luckily Mum stayed with me. Madge gave me something to stop the vomiting, but I felt very sick all night, in spite of the medicine. When morning came, I was exhausted, and I was just going to sleep at last when Denise arrived. "It's breakfast time," she called cheerfully.

"You must be kidding," I said. "I've been as sick as a dog all night, please don't talk to me about food!" But she insisted and I managed to drink some herb tea and eat some dry biscuits.

8

At times I felt terribly depressed and I often cried. "Take it one day at a time," Mum advised me with a loving smile. "You'll see you can put up with much more than you think." I stopped crying. Another day of chemo was about to start for me, and I would have preferred to be anywhere else in the world rather than in this hospital, but I decided to be courageous. In the course of those days all the hospital routines followed each other relentlessly, and the hours stretched out interminably. Moments of great impatience alternated with periods of powerless passivity. I was learning patience! I wanted to cry, but I tried to be brave. My parents watched out for the slightest change of expression on my face, which did not make things any easier. I would have liked to cry alone in my corner, but I was never alone. At the same time, I was relieved to have them there. All this was very confusing and contradictory in my mind. Nausea came over me at unforeseeable intervals, and each time I coped with it less well. When the sick feeling became too strong, I finally managed to vomit and that was a real relief, even though it was exhausting since there wasn't much in my stomach. But the relief was short lived, and it all started again. I often asked for something to take, I who hate medicines. The days seemed at the same time endless and yet short, because the evening would come without my having done anything apart from receive my dose of chemo, vomit, snooze, and complain. I was learning yet another lesson: in hospital, time doesn't pass in the same way as in ordinary life. I had no landmarks, even with regard to the passing of the day. That is probably why I felt so lost.

The days followed one another and were all the same. As soon as I felt a bit better, I would go into the common room. I had got quite used to the bald heads of the children and teenagers.

Denise was right. It wasn't very beautiful, that's for sure, but it no longer frightened me. There were Christian, Mark and, above all, Susan who was so joyful and kind that everybody liked her immediately. The discussions we had were mainly about our various illnesses. There were five of us suffering from acute lymphoblastic leukaemia, A.L.L. as they call it. The others had other types of cancer. I was discovering a new world. First of all, the solidarity. You could see they were very close, and the older ones were kind to the little ones. I learned a lot about my illness from being with them. Sometimes the conversations turned towards our life before the illness, our life "outside", and it did us good to talk about something other than illness. Hope and anguish came over me alternately, and it was exhausting. How the illness developed was one of the favourite topics in our little group. We all knew that our future depended on it, and we tried to see it clearly. The "elders", that is to say those who had already been in for a long time, were our teachers. By gleaning information from doctors, nurses, laboratory assistants and parents, they had become real specialists in cancer and its treatment. But what they said no doubt also contained some confused ideas and errors, and I didn't always believe them. For instance, when Christian said that the more chemo you have, the more likely you are to die, I refused to believe him. It couldn't be like that, because the chemo kills the diseased cells and cures us. As soon as Denise came back from her lunch break, I asked her to explain. I was sure that she would burst out laughing as she often does and say, "Of course not, Christian has got it all wrong, chemo cures children. The more you have, the more chance you have of getting better quickly." But she said nothing of the sort. She remained evasive, which is really not like her, and that made me very frightened. So, I went back to Christian and asked him to explain. "It's because the body can't stand more than a certain dose of chemo. Beyond a certain amount the medication might attack the heart or the kidneys, and we could die from the secondary effects of the treatment," he told me sadly. "We're all waiting for them to hurry up and find other types of medicine, but since it is very complicated, it takes a long time. I hope we won't die before they find out, that would really be too stupid!" I felt an icy cold seize hold of me. So, wasn't it really a race against time? Not only was the chemo hard to bear because it made us so sick, but it did not even guarantee a cure? I turned on my heel and went to my room to cry. I felt angry with Christian for having told me. I would have preferred him to let me believe that the chemo was successful in all cases and that we would all get better soon. I decided to stay in my room more often and to talk less to children who knew too much.

~

Two weeks had passed and I was still in hospital. I had spent my days receiving my dose of chemo, struggling with nausea, vomiting frequently, sleeping often, and crying a lot. My parents took it in turns to stay at my bedside when I was too tired to go and see my new friends. When I felt a bit better, I went to the common room to watch videos or television with the others or listen to music. There were also video games and even a machine for recharging mobile telephones because young people do a lot of phoning. There was everything to entertain us and to give us pleasure, we appreciated it, but even so, it wasn't a holiday camp! We began to get very close in spite of the age differences, and we were happy to be together. There were some people who annoyed me a bit, but that wasn't important. They helped to take my mind off my anxiety, my worry and distress, and made me forget for a little while that I felt sick all the time. What's more I realized that my turmoil was alleviated for a brief moment when we all talked together about our illness. Their bald heads no longer bothered me at all, but I was very happy not to have the same problem as them, because my long hair was as beautiful as ever.

~

At the beginning of the third week something horrible happened: Susan died. I didn't know her very well. She had just come back to hospital because of a complication following her chemo. For a week she had hardly ever left her room, but then for a few days she had often joined us in the common room. She was very pleased to be feeling better, and she told us about a trip to Spain that she was taking the following month with her parents and one of her friends. She was a bit older than me and so cheerful that it made you want to be friends with her. We had some talks and played cards once. It seemed she had had a haemorrhage the night before. I didn't really understand what had happened. Mark told me that there was blood everywhere and that it was horrible. Susan's mother had become completely hysterical when she saw her daughter die. She had screamed in the corridor. The night duty team had tried to calm her and take her into the nurses' room. They wanted to stop her waking us all up. I hadn't heard anything because I was sound asleep. I don't know where Mark had got all this information from, but it's true that he was usually very well informed. So, Susan won't be going to Spain after all with her parents and her friend, or anywhere else for that matter. In my sadness I told myself that we were all going to end up like her. I was tired of being so unhappy.

9

That evening I was lying in the half-light of my room, lit only by the glow of my bedside lamp. I cuddled Angel in my arms, holding her tightly against me, as I had become accustomed to doing ever since I had been in hospital. With my eyes closed I thought of Susan, her cheerful laughter and her blue eyes sparkling with fun the last time I had seen her. She was so glad to be leaving hospital in the near future, I could feel so strongly her desire to return to normal life, her home, her family, her friends, and her dog. It was the same for all of us, leaving hospital became an obsession, symbolizing a door opening into freedom, a promise of the future, the deliverance from this nightmare which had intruded so brutally into our peaceful happy lives. I was wondering about the haemorrhage that had killed her, and I imagined her blood spread all over the place. I wondered where the blood might have come from, and that reminded me of my nosebleed when we were on holiday on the island of Zakynthos. An icy terror gripped me. And what if my nose started to bleed again, and I died of it? At that moment I felt a warmth on my chest as if I were on a beach exposed to the full heat of the sun. I opened my eyes and saw an intense warm light coming from Angel as she lay on my chest. At first, I was afraid. There was something supernatural in this light coming from my doll. I thought of my grandmother who had knitted her for me, and immediately I felt reassured. Nothing strange or worrying could come from her. I knew that I was going to be able to talk with my favourite doll and there again was nothing to be frightened of. I had talked to her so often in the past, and especially since I had been in hospital, so it was natural for her to answer me. I wasn't even sure that this was particularly original. All dolls can talk if they are loved enough. In tears I told her that Susan's death had made me very sad, and then a dialogue began.

"I miss Susan so much," I said with a sob, "she was so cheerful... we got on really well. She had leukaemia like me and she's died, that means I can die of it too. I don't think I've ever been so unhappy in all my life."

Angel answered:

"Death is always sad for those who are left behind."

"And especially for those who die! I can imagine her under the earth, buried in a coffin, all alone in the dark and cold. All the time I can see a cemetery, and I can see the shadows moving, I can hear frightening noises in the dark and I would like to run to her and hold her hand. But I suppose that hand is now cold, perhaps even decomposing, eaten by worms... It is horrible, Angel, this idea is haunting me all the time."

"What you are describing is truly horrible, but maybe things don't really happen like that. Imagine that Susan still exists somewhere else without her body..."

"Without her body? How could that be possible?"

"Try to imagine that she has left her body and floated away."

"How do you mean, left her body... I don't understand."

Angel said with her mischievous smile which I was the only one able to notice on her dolly face:

"The idea might seem strange, I agree, but it's quite simple. Let's take you as an example. Imagine that, when you die, you escape from your body, but still remain yourself. You will see this body from the outside, from a certain distance above it, and you will not be sad to have left it behind because it no longer means anything to you. Dazzled you will wonder how it is possible to feel so well, so happy, so free, so entirely and completely yourself, in spite of, or perhaps because of, the separation from your body which is lying beneath you. You will notice in astonishment and delight that you have kept your personality, your identity, your character. Your earthly life will indeed be present, but already less important, like a memory gently fading... What was is, and will remain. You will stay the same, with your feelings intact but slightly detached from your life history which will, however, form your new existence. In a state of wonder you will find yourself enjoying new and powerful emotions linked to your new state, infinitely greater than the rather dull feelings that you had during your earthly life. You will be overwhelmed by this new state of being, so strange and yet so wonderful, which will give you an uplifting vision and understanding of the human reality. I assure you that you won't for a second regret your body that you are leaving behind, like some old clothes that you no longer need."

Intrigued, I insisted:

"I still don't understand. I'm one with my body, I am my body. Without my body, I'm nothing, I don't exist anymore."

"That's just an illusion. What you are saying seems right and sensible, but it really is too simplistic. I agree with you, it's very difficult to imagine yourself without a body. However, if you look at it differently, if you consider it from another angle, I'm sure the evidence speaks for itself. But you have been conditioned by one single way of thinking, just as you have been imprisoned within your body. Just imagine that you will be yourself, but without your body."

"You say 'without your body' but that's exactly what I cannot understand."

"Imagine that people are like caterpillars. When they begin the transformation into chrysalis, one would think that their old, visible form dies. But that is not so! In reality, they change into butterflies. When the time has come for them to take on another form of expression, they simply leave their old envelope behind and fly toward a new and completely different existence. Do you now understand any better this separation of consciousness — or soul if you prefer to call it that — from the body?"

"I understand that for the butterfly but not for me. It's natural for a butterfly to fly, but I wouldn't be able to because I haven't got any wings."

"It is an image to illustrate something that I can't explain in simple terms because it is very different from what you know. So, I'm talking about a butterfly flying away, but really, I mean that it is *you* who flies away, you without your body, you as a unique and immortal being."

Irritated, I said:

"I'd like to understand you because I find what you're describing both pleasing and attractive, but it's so complicated..."

"No, not really... Let's invent a game together, the game of the 'absolute being'. Let's pretend it's true and let's go into a magic world... Imagine that, on earth, you are only one of the multiple—maybe even infinite—forms of expression, or facets, of your 'absolute being'. Your life on earth is only one of its possible forms of existence.

"The absolute being exists already and takes shape—in its form of expression as a human being—temporarily in a physical body which will be abandoned again at the moment of 'death', so that the absolute being can take on another of its possible forms of expression. That means that the true nature of the absolute being always remains unchanged. Each of these forms of expression is therefore 'true', real and consistent and can be observed in its respective environment. 'Death' can therefore be seen as a transitory process which enables the absolute being to take on yet another of its forms of expression and, by doing so, to 'activate' another of its possible facets.

"By dying, the human beings change their form of expression, but they do not cease to exist. Of course, to each of the forms of expression of the absolute being belong certain characteristics. According to which form of expression has been taken on, you can experiment and use the respective possibilities and abilities. Who knows, maybe the form of expression as a human being is the one with the most limited and restricted abilities and possibilities?

"And imagine... when human beings leave their body and take on another form of expression, they reach a dimension where material restrictions no longer exist. Space and time are abolished and beings can move to any point in space in no time and without any difficulty.

"In fact, they do not 'move' since this term is characterized by time passing, they just *are* all at once in a different place. Maybe you don't even need an external form of expression anymore in this new dimension, as this is probably only necessary as long as you are a human being in this world.

"Who knows which form of expression you will take on and what possibilities of perception you will have when you will leave the state of a human being?

"Now you must rest, we will talk about it again tomorrow..."

~

The next day I told myself in astonishment that you can get used to anything, even spending your holidays in a university hospital, a long way from home, in an ugly room, surrounded by cheerful nurses and sick children. In fact, the phrase "get used to" was probably ill-chosen: it would perhaps have been better to say that you adapt because you have to; you put up with it because you haven't the option of refusing, of saying "No, thank you," and going home.

I thought over what Angel had said all day, and in the evening as soon as the light was out in my room, I continued my conversation with her.

"Angel, last night you explained to me that people who are on the point of dying leave their bodies and fly away like butterflies, but what is it that is separated from the body?"

"The soul, the consciousness, the spirit, different terms are used for the same idea. What do these words mean? The difficulty in understanding them comes from the fact that you never think of yourself without your body. You probably imagine that your thoughts are formed in your brain, that your memories are stored away somewhere, and that your feelings originate in your heart, as does the love that you feel. But there is nothing to prove that this is actually the case. Imagine a different scenario: let's agree that consciousness enters the body of the foetus when it is in the mother's womb. For the whole life of this foetus—which will become a baby, then a child, an adolescent and then an adult, and finally an old person—consciousness is rooted in the body. So human beings think logically that they and their body are one, but the truth is that when they die, when their *body* dies—they themselves don't die—they leave their body just as simply as they entered it at the moment of conception. Plato, the famous Greek philosopher, said that the soul—or the consciousness—returns to its place of origin at the moment of death. The problem is that human beings don't remember anything at the time of their birth, nor afterwards. For the whole of their life, they will try to find a knowledge that they possessed before birth, that they carry hidden in the deepest part of themselves, but the content of which they have forgotten. They will try to solve the mystery of life and death, the enigma of the human condition, the fate of their being after the death of the body. Plato said that reflection, philosophy and experience will help them gradually to remember at least part of it. Seen from this angle, does the idea of the separation of consciousness from the body seem simpler to you?"

"It's not very easy to imagine, but I understand the idea a bit better. However, that doesn't resolve the problem that Susan's body is in its box under the earth and that it's probably being eaten by worms."

"I think the talk about worms is more myth than reality, but even so, what does it matter since the body is no longer inhabited?"

"Even so, it is frightening!"

"If you reason it out, you'll have to admit that the body is like a garment which is abandoned at the moment when consciousness flies away towards its new destiny. So, who would worry about some old clothes?"

10

I had spent the whole evening lying stock still in my bed, puzzled and enchanted at the same time. I didn't even want to watch the television because a much more interesting story than any film, even a mystery film, was going round in my head: a life without a body, an existence in another world, a hope beyond unhappiness... That was a lot to think about.

For several days I had realized that I was waiting impatiently for the evening to come so that I could continue my discussions with Angel. What she was telling me was answering questions that were coming from deep down inside me. Even if I didn't understand all that she was saying, her words intrigued and reassured me at the same time. Although I was delighted to talk to my new friends during the day, I realized that we were all at the same point: lots of questions and no answers. With Angel it was different; Angel knew. Although I had been asleep all afternoon, that evening I was so tired that my head was spinning. All the same I had decided to ask Angel a crucial question, one which had been tormenting me since the beginning of my illness.

"Angel, why did I become ill? Why me?"

"The individual destiny forms part of a greater plan which is difficult to understand. All I can tell you is that nothing happens by chance and that everything has a meaning."

"And what meaning could this leukaemia possibly have for me? I find what you say rather shocking!"

"It will probably help you to grow."

"To grow... physically?"

"No, not physically, but as a person."

"Professor Granger said something like that too, that illness is a source of growth and enrichment for the patient and the family... but it's easy to say that when you're healthy."

"No, on the contrary it is very difficult because the injustice of it all seems so great. You want to find the right words, to offer comfort and be able to justify it all."

"So, you're suggesting that I ought to be grateful for being ill, so I can grow as a person?"

"No, illness and suffering are always an unbearable injustice, there is nothing positive to be said about them and in themselves they can teach us nothing at all. It all depends on what the person suffering makes of it, if they manage to be strong enough to turn the ordeal into a lesson in living. Courage and willpower will be their most precious allies, which will help to overcome their fragility with a life force which will sublimate it."

"I don't feel strong at all, I've got a knot in my stomach all the time, and at night I'm very frightened. I think about what will happen to me and about the children who died."

"Of course, you are facing the harsh realities of life and yet you are so young. Thinking deeply about it will help you through your illness, and you have the courage to ask the right questions. You don't hide behind illusions but instead you dare to confront the reality of your situation. What's more you aren't alone: there are your parents, the nurses, the sick children."

"It's true that I feel all right with my new friends. We all have the same problems, the same distress, the same hope and we understand one another without even saying anything. We are happy to be together, in spite of our physical problems, as if we had *decided* to be happy, contrary to all expectations, even though it goes against common sense."

"That's another wonderful weapon that you have: joy! It is without doubt the ultimate expression of courage to be happy in spite of everything, what a challenge! You rise above your illness in those moments of happiness, and against all the odds life comes out on top."

"But I feel so fragile."

"Yes, you have to rely on the doctors, the nurses, the various treatments, that's true. But the force of your will stands up against the fragility of your body. You have the freedom to try to get out of this trial in spite of your unhappiness. Everything is going wrong, but it is precisely this hardship which will show how strong you are. The illness has no hold over the attitude that you decide to adopt: give way or struggle, the decision is yours."

"I don't really seem to be fighting but rather submitting to events, the days that come one after the other with their share of treatment, discomfort, waiting and boredom. Yes, it's probably boredom which is the hardest to bear, and also the impression that life is happening somewhere else, and I'm cut off from it."

"Courage assumes many different guises. While you have the will to face each new day optimistically, to go ahead despite your unhappiness, to provide for yourself a little breathing space and a few moments of joy in these painful wearisome days, that way you will win, you will not have given up, you will not have laid down your arms, you will have succeeded in exercising your freedom."

"There are moments when I don't know how to go on, how to bear it all, who to turn to for comfort."

"The answer is within yourself. In spite of the gloominess of your situation, you can decide how to colour your days. In spite of your problems, in spite of your distress, you are free to form your everyday life as you choose, beyond the restrictions of your body, because your spirit is indomitable. The world takes on the face that you draw for it, your thoughts create reality despite your illness, despite the uncertainty of your future."

11

It was Sunday and my parents brought my friend Nicole who had just come back from her horse-riding holiday. She was visibly shaken and very ill at ease. Her eyes betrayed her confusion, even though she made a great effort to hide it. Since she was reluctant to ask me about my illness, she launched into an incoherent, boring description of her holiday. I suppose she was also embarrassed because my parents were there; normally when she came to our house, we would go into my bedroom or the garden. She had picked up Angel and was fiddling with her nervously. I didn't like to see her messing around with my doll, and I wanted to take it away, but I didn't do anything about it. My parents tried to put us at our ease by livening up the conversation, but that made things even worse. If they had left us alone, perhaps the ice would have been broken, but I'm not sure about that. I had the impression that Nicole was afraid of being left on her own talking to me. So, contrary to my expectations, this visit gave me no pleasure at all and, like Nicole, I felt relieved when my parents decided to put an end to the visit and take her home. Once I was alone, I wanted to hug Angel, but then I realized she had disappeared. In a panic I looked everywhere for her, in the bed, on the bedside table, on the radiator shelf which I used as a place to keep things as I did with the table at the other end of the room. No sign of Angel.

I put on my dressing gown and slippers and ran into the corridor. At the end of the corridor there was a window that looked out onto the car park. I reached it just in time to see my parents and Nicole walking towards our car.

Had Nicole taken Angel away with her without thinking? No, she hadn't got anything in her hands. Dumbfounded I went back to my room, and as soon as I got into the doorway, I saw Angel under the bed. Nicole must have dropped her as she got up. Relieved, I told myself that I would never let anyone play with my doll ever again. I knelt down to reach her and got back into bed. I thought over Nicole's visit and told myself that, oddly, I felt more at ease with my sick friends who I had only known for such a short time. We had something in common, the main thing in fact, our cancer, our distress, and our uncertain hopes of recovery.

~

That morning wasn't an ordinary morning, if you can class as ordinary all the other mornings that I spent in the University Hospital, Department of Paediatric Oncology, which is the correct name for it. Let's say that in an unusual period of my life, it was an exceptional morning: my last day of chemo had arrived. I was full of joy and anguish at the same time because the next day I would have to have a biopsy to determine whether I was in remission. Remission doesn't mean cure, I knew that very well, but it was the initial stage of it, the first step towards freedom. There was another great anxiety in addition to the fear of the biopsy: I was losing my hair in handfuls! An obscure fear had been haunting me ever since the first moment I had seen those sick children, bald and pale. This question that I had obstinately refused to face up to had finally been answered: yes, I was losing my hair too, yes, I too was going to frighten children who were healthy and perhaps adults as well. Gradually, my initial joy disappeared and I felt dejected and sad. I had a knot in my stomach and was aware that I was only breathing superficially and that sometimes I couldn't take a proper breath. I finally realized this and breathed in deeply which made me give deep sighs. All this made me have a headache which upset me even more.

~

The next morning the preparations for the biopsy of the bone marrow didn't go at all well. Professor Granger and a nurse called Fiona whom I didn't know certainly did all they could to calm me down, but in spite of their efforts I was terribly stressed and tense during the preparation for the anaesthetic. When I woke up from the anaesthetic, I thought I was going to feel better at last, but this wasn't the case. The worry about my hair was with me all the time. In fact, it was worse than a worry, more like suffering, torment, mourning. I realized how beautiful my hair was, long and silky. It was just as I was losing it that I loved it most. I panicked at the idea that on my bald head I too would have bumps that would make me look like a monster. That night I had a terrible nightmare in which demons, witches and sick children were chasing one another, intertwined and merged. It was horrible and I woke up at about four in the morning sweating and terrified. I didn't manage to get back to sleep and it was in a state of terror that I waited for the dawn.

In the morning Professor Granger was due to come to give us the results of the biopsy and to announce my remission. Dad had taken the day off work so that he could be with Mum and me to receive the good news — but it was bad! I understood this as soon as I saw the doctor's face. The answer was clearly written there. I told myself I was starting to get to know him so well that I could read his thoughts easily. Today I think he intentionally allowed his sadness to appear on his face, this genuine sorrow at not being able to do more, to look after me better, to cure me more quickly. So, the bad news was communicated to me on two levels of consciousness. First of all, stealthily, almost instinctively, followed by these terrible words: "I'm very sorry but there are still some malignant cells left. The treatment hasn't eradicated all the diseased cells, we shall have to prolong the chemotherapy."

"No!" I heard myself yelling this word which came back to hit me like a slap in the face. "I can't put up with any more weeks like this, not even a single day! I can't bear it! I don't want to; I want to go home!" I burst into sobs, overcome with the deepest despair and I was seized by a violent bout of hiccups which I couldn't control. What a life! What a summer! What a nightmare! I buried my face in the pillow and wrapped my arms around my head so as not to hear any more. Mum turned me round towards her tenderly and with infinite sadness. With a movement of her hand, she gently moved aside my fringe which was soaked in sweat and sticking to my forehead, then she stopped suddenly. She was holding in her fingers a lock of my hair which had come out. "I'm falling apart!" I told myself, seized with an indescribable terror. My tears stopped dead. The horror was so intense that it was even depriving me of the comfort of tears and sobs to ease the tension. An icy cold sensation came over me and again I had difficulty in breathing. "I would do better to stop breathing for good," I told myself, "in any case, it isn't doing any good. I'm falling apart and I shall end up dying anyway."

~

I spent the rest of the day like a zombie, completely divorced from reality, enclosed in my terror. Not only was I frantic at the thought of having to face more chemotherapy, but equally overwhelmed by the thought of the extra dose of medication that my body would have to cope with. If Christian had left me under the illusion that more chemo meant a quicker recovery, I would no doubt have taken this bad news better, but he had explained to me that the secondary effects of chemo could kill us. Denise hadn't contradicted Christian's words, and I couldn't act as if I didn't know—I *did* know! I wondered as well why the chemo hadn't eradicated all my diseased cells.

The next morning, I asked my friends, but this time no one could give me a satisfactory answer. Either they didn't know, or else my case was serious and no one wanted to tell me. Although I was terribly frightened of the answer, all the same I wanted to know why it was necessary to prolong the treatment. I asked Agnes if I could go to the hospital library. She must have suspected that I had some motive for this, but since the philosophy of the carers demands the maximum honesty in dealing with patients who are kept fully informed of the state of their health—as Mum very elegantly put it—Agnes told me where the library was without asking any questions. I had no problem finding the information I was looking for in a medical dictionary under the heading of "Acute Lymphoblastic Leukaemia" and in the chapter "Treatment of the Illness": *A poor response to the induction treatment suggests a poor prognosis.* As the meaning of these words penetrated my mind, I understood that I could really die of my leukaemia. From the time of the diagnosis of my illness I had been in the grip of a vague anguish which hadn't left me for a second and was present even during those rare moments when a brief feeling of joy or pleasure came over me. This distress was with me in the daytime and especially at night, but it had never been expressed so clearly: *A poor response to the induction treatment suggests a poor prognosis.* It was the saddest sentence I had ever read.

~

Professor Granger heard I had been to consult books in the library and obviously deduced from this that I needed more information. Therefore, he organized a visit to the lab technician who worked for our department so she could show me my blood sample and explain to me all I wanted to know about my illness. I appreciated the steps he had taken because it was my blood, my body, my illness, therefore my responsibility. The lab technician, who was called Beatrice, was quite an old woman, with grey hair cut short, and who wore glasses with thick lenses. I concluded from this that she had ruined her eyesight by looking through her microscope, but she dispelled this idea by showing me with a big smile lots of apparatus, centrifuges, and other strange machines. She explained to me that the traditional microscope had been largely replaced by much more reliable instruments. Then she fetched a sample of blood bearing my name and slipped it into a machine which didn't look like anything I knew. She asked me to sit down while she pressed the button to switch it on. What I saw looked like pebbles of different shapes, placed one against the other, overlapping in places. The pebbles were separated by fragments which looked like grains of sand. All this reminded me in an odd way of a beach at the seaside. Beatrice explained to me the anomalies in the makeup of my blood. I told myself that the cancerous cells were quite pretty to look at and that their appearance didn't go along with such a dreadful illness.

12

I had a question to put to Angel, an important question, and I waited until she was willing to talk to me. At last, the next evening this happened and I asked her:

"What makes people get ill and die?"

"Life is a collection of happy and sorrowful events. Human beings are confronted by a whole lot of situations, one of which is illness, which they have to cope with as best they can. Some people think that these events happen in a random way, quite by chance, others believe they are part of a greater plan."

"This greater plan as you call it, is it God?"

"You can call it that."

"If God exists, how can He allow children to become ill and die?"

"In one sentence you are asking the fundamental questions which have always preoccupied human beings: does God exist, and if so, how can He allow injustice to occur? Let's start at the beginning... Do you believe in God?"

"I don't know. When I was little, I believed in Him. I imagined Him in the sky sitting on a cloud: I think I got that idea from a book that Mum read to me. Since I've been ill, I'm not so sure... I say my prayers every evening like I used to, but now my prayers are no longer about an exam at school that I'm frightened about or a problem with my friends. Today I only ask for one thing—to get better! When my grandmother turned ill, I prayed for her a lot but she died all the same. I don't know if I can trust Him..."

"Praying shouldn't consist of asking for something, but rather of coming into contact with God."

"I don't know how to do that, I'm not even sure that He exists."

"He cannot exist for you unless you open the door to Him, unless you let Him enter your heart. It's you who creates your reality, it's you who decides..."

"I don't understand, either He exists or He doesn't exist, that doesn't depend on me."

"Oh yes, it does... Each time you think of Him, each time you believe in Him, you make Him exist a bit more in your universe. Give yourself the means of believing in Him."

"I didn't think He was really sitting on a cloud in the sky, but where is He?"

"He is inside you if you decide that is the case, He is all around you, He is in each human being, He is everywhere, He reveals Himself each time someone makes Him exist."

"What can I do to talk to Him?"

"You talk to Him as you are talking to me, in your heart, in all simplicity, in all intimacy."

"How will I know He's listening to me?"

"You will know because you will feel less alone."

"Haven't I the right to ask Him to cure me?"

"You have the right to ask Him whatever you wish, that takes place between you and yourself, between you and Him, that's personal."

"What's the use of prayer?"

"If you stick to the idea that God is the great conductor of the orchestra, prayer will help you to understand the situations that He makes you experience and to accept more easily the illness that has come into your life."

"If I pray hard enough and often enough, I'll get better, is that it?"

"It's more complicated than that..."

"So, God cures some children and lets others die, and He is called the good God...?"

"The answer to your question, or rather your protest, probably lies in trust. Trust in life, trust in your destiny, so in the end trust in God. In fact, it's a question of your point of view. Human beings haven't got access to the whole picture, they can only see a tiny part of it, which makes no sense, which is incoherent, even absurd. With humility they must accept that they don't know, that they cannot understand, that they aren't in possession of the whole picture. But the decision is yours. In spite of your feelings of protest, in spite of your suffering, in spite of your fear, you are still free to trust or not."

"All that's so complicated, the picture that I can't see, the choices I have to make all the time... Can you explain it any better?"

"Yes, I suggest we continue our game which focuses on the idea of the absolute being. We have decided that this being would have lots of facets or forms of expression. When we say that, we aren't being quite accurate because when one is absolute, one has no limits, one is by nature plural and universal. But we don't want to make the rules of the game too complicated, right? So, let's imagine that this absolute being exists, then takes on a body as a human being, then, at the moment of its physical death, it becomes disembodied to take on another of its many facets or forms of expression. Intrinsically the nature of the absolute being remains unchanged, although its forms of expression are characterized by more or less powerful properties.

"We decided that each of its facets — or forms of expression — would be 'true', consistent and observable in a given context. Thus, in the context of 'living on Earth', you would perceive the 'human' facet with its reality of a woman or a man living their life on Earth, going through all the necessary stages like birth, childhood, adolescence, adulthood—with their share of joy and sorrow—then comes illness, and finally 'death'. So, death would be a transitory process, like birth, which would allow the human being to pass into another dimension, and, by doing so, to activate another of its possible forms of expression.

"By dying, the human beings become 'other', they do not cease to exist. They change their state—but not their nature. Are you following the ideas of the game?"

"I think so, yes, I think I understand... so the human being would only be one of the possible forms of expression of the absolute being, of its 'facets' I think you called them also... By dying, it changes its state... like water which can be liquid, steam or turn into ice, would that be a good comparison?"

"That's a perfect example. Water can be liquid, vaporous or solid. It changes from one state to the other by melting, evaporating or freezing, and yet it remains water."

"So, according to where you are, you can see certain things and not others?"

"Exactly. Depending on the state you are in, you are able to see certain things... or not. Each one of the forms of expression — or facets—of the absolute being has its own reality, but which can only be observed and understood in that dimension.

"Let's take another simple example. From the valley, you can only see a small part of your environment, for example, the fields around you and perhaps the forest on the mountainside. If, on the other hand, you climb up to the summit of the mountain, then you will see the whole valley dotted with small villages, decorated with little rivers which wind their way to the horizon and you might even notice a town in the distance. From the top of the mountain, you will have a wider perception of the valley, and you will understand better the lie of the land, why one river could only follow the course it took, because of the level of the terrain, the presence of the hills or other natural obstacles. From up there, all this will be very clear."

"I can understand all that fine, but what has it got to do with my illness?"

"It's directly connected: you are asking bitter but justifiable questions about the reasons for your illness, but you must accept that human beings don't have at their disposal the broad perspective which would allow them to understand the course of their life, the sense of their suffering, the design of their destiny, because they are in the valley... When they change their state and pass into another dimension—when they change their form of expression—then they will stand at the top of the mountain, and will contemplate their earthly existence from a wider point of view. By abandoning their body and their human condition, they will enter a new dimension which will reveal to them in a flash of understanding the reason for all the events in their earthly life."

"How is that going to be of any real help to me in coping with my illness?"

"All your doubts about your illness, the question why you cannot always be in good health, the mystery of the 'will of God', all these questions are relevant from the perspective of human beings. But when you look at yourself from the absolute point of view, which corresponds to what you really are, that is, an absolute being, then these questions cease to be relevant. Now that we have invented the magic world of the absolute being, you hold the key which opens the door to the understanding of your life from a completely new perspective. The rest is a path which you can follow with trust."

That night I stayed awake a very long time, delighted, trying to remember all the things Angel had said which were complicated and clear at the same time. Sliding gently in the realm of sleep, I dreamed of snow-covered peaks and golden rivers.

13

Some days later, lying in the half-light, I was awaiting the arrival of Sarah, the night nurse who started her duty at 10 pm. I waited another half hour before pressing the call button installed above my bed.

When Mum had found herself with a handful of my hair in her hand, I had taken an important decision, a firm decision. I was going to have my head shaved! I couldn't go on leaving hair everywhere, on my pillow, in the hairbrush, in the shower... everywhere! My beautiful hair was starting to get thin in places, and that I couldn't bear. It was too sad, better to be bald all at once. I didn't have the courage to shave it myself; anyway, I didn't have any means of doing it. Neither did I want to talk about it to my parents, because, like me, they were involved and sad. No, only Sarah could help me by taking the drama out of this act which symbolized my fragility and my decline, but no doubt she wouldn't see things that way. She was capable of telling me that my hair would grow again, and that there really was no need to get into such a state for a few locks of hair. Those were exactly the words that I needed to hear. I rang and a few minutes later the door opened and Sarah appeared. "Hello, my pet, what's happening?" she asked with a smile.

"I'm losing my hair and I want it shaved off," I replied.

"Okay," she said without the slightest astonishment. "I'll go and fetch what we need." She came back straightaway with a sort of razor that I had seen at our hairdresser's and she settled me down in the armchair in the corner of the room. After she put a towel around my shoulders, she switched on the razor. It was then that I burst into sobs. "I don't want to look like a monster, Sarah, I shall frighten everybody, and especially myself!" It's true that I had got used to seeing my friends with their bare heads, but when it was my own head, it was quite different. "But you won't frighten anyone, what are you thinking of?" she answered. "Look, do you feel sad when you cut your fingernails?"

"No," I replied, "but I don't see the connection."

"You cut your nails and they grow again, you cut your hair and it grows again in the same way, it's the same idea," replied Sarah with conviction. I found the comparison absolutely stupid, but at the same time I was touched by Sarah's well-meaning words, and her efforts, which weren't always successful, to take the drama out of a difficult situation. "You're right," I said with a smile. I then saw the look of astonishment on her face, because she was expecting me to protest and was already preparing in her mind for the argument to follow. She looked at me closely and understood that, far from having convinced me, she had touched me and that in that case the words had no importance—I was suffering, and she was feeling for me. "Let's get this done," she said in a husky voice. I felt the razor moving around on my head while the hair fell on to my shoulders and my arms. "You're facing huge difficulties," she said, "difficulties you shouldn't have to cope with at your age. The best way of getting through the trial is to face it with courage, and you certainly have lots of it." The razor made a snapping sound when Sarah stopped. She took away the towel. I stood up and Sarah put her arm round my shoulders, then we went to the bathroom. I had carefully avoided looking at my hair spread out on the floor. Although I had sworn to myself I would treat the matter lightly, in spite of all that, I felt a shock at the sight of my reflection in the mirror. My eyes, which looked enormous, brought out the pallor of my face, and I was astonished to see that my ears were large and sticking out. I looked exactly like the bald children who had frightened me so much the day I got to know them. I dreaded having bumps on my head, and I asked Sarah to fetch a mirror. I wanted to see the back of my head. Sarah came back quickly with a little mirror, and I looked at my head for bumps.

Thank God there were none. "Your head is a very nice shape," said Sarah, stroking my cheek. I put down the little mirror and inspected myself again in the mirror above the washbasin. Without any hair my head looked smaller, more bare, exposed to other people's stares, the symbol of my vulnerability. It was frightening, but that was how it was, and I was going to have to accept it. I had entered a new stage in the course of my illness.

Sarah had left me, and I was getting ready to go to sleep, exhausted by so many emotions. As a habit, at the moment I went to sleep, I would turn to my side and automatically push my hair away from my face. That night, as I was falling asleep, I tried to push back my hair away from my face as usual, when I realized that there was nothing there anymore, and that was terrible. I sobbed myself to sleep.

~

The next morning, I was in the corridor going towards the common room when I saw Mum coming. It was scary to see her like this, caught off guard, so to speak. In my presence she was always full of smiles, making superhuman efforts to hide her sadness, her distress, her tiredness. I was now the most important thing in her life, everything revolved around me, she would have been ready to give her own life to save mine. What's more, her smile and her never ending gentleness always managed to give me a feeling of comfort. The strength of her love kept me anchored to life. Seeing her like this, with her face tense, looking ten years older in the space of a few weeks, I realized that one day she would die too. To see her looking so fragile and in such despair filled me with great sadness. She was walking very fast, giving me a vacant glance as she passed me by as she made her way towards my room. "Mum, Mum, it's me!" I said as I caught up with her. Even my own mother doesn't recognize me with no hair, I thought in shock. She turned and gave a little cry. But her wonderful smile full of love at once lit up her face. She put her arms round me, and we stayed like this for a long time, crying. Those were good tears, tears which give relief and comfort. When there are two of you and you love each other, you can put up with anything.

~

A few days later, Angel decided to talk to me at last. I had been waiting for this moment for a long time. A multitude of questions were buzzing around in my head, and Angel was the only one who could answer them.

"These last few days I've often been upset by the way people look at me. Since I lost my hair, everyone can see that I'm ill. I feel exposed and I would really like not to be noticed. Some people smile at me, others look away, but nobody is natural. It's true that my appearance has changed, but inside, I'm the same person. I'm upset by the fear that I cause in certain people. It's as if I frighten myself when I see their reaction to me."

"It's the illness that causes fear and the way other people look at you adds to the distress instead of easing it."

"It's true, I had a shock myself the first time I met the sick children. I remember I ran into my room and threw myself on the bed, sobbing. Now I'm like them..."

"You have gone over to the other side, to their side, you know now that there is no reason at all to be afraid of them. Through your illness you have been thrust into the world of people who are different."

"Why is difference so frightening?"

"It is the fear of the unknown, it comes from a lack of information and above all, from a lack of contact. As soon as someone decides to go to meet the other person, to enter their universe, one discovers the person, one disregards the difference. Behind the dissimilarity one finds a human being in all their complexity, in their uniqueness, also in their splendour. There may or may not be fellow feeling, but at least this choice will be made for good reasons."

"Now I feel closer to people who are different. In my class there was a very fat girl, everybody called her the elephant, and that made her cry. I can understand now how she must have felt."

"Yes, many people experience this type of exclusion. People have a tendency to seek out those who are like themselves, when there is richness to be gained from diversity."

"I have the impression that I've learned a lot since I became ill."

"You learn from misfortune, and you are growing up... Do you remember our conversation the other evening, when you asked me why this illness had come into your life?"

"Of course, and you told me that it would make me grow as a person, but I'm still not sure that I agree with you. I rather have the impression that I'm completely passive, submitted to this body which gives me so much trouble, and which is examined, injected, subjected to drips, X-rayed and washed as if I were a thing. I can't see what I have to do to grow as a person."

"In only a few weeks, you have discovered how precious life is. You have realized the fragility of your body, and the consequences of the imbalance of cells which has upset your whole system. Through the distress and fear caused by your state of health, you became aware of the splendour of this sophisticated machine which is the human body, which struggles constantly against external and internal aggressions, rebalancing itself and renewing itself ceaselessly in a dizzy ballet which is infinitely well choreographed. You will never forget this lesson."

"Perhaps so, but for the moment, I think only of my illness, and I find it so unfair!"

"You could let yourself be carried away by anger and the feeling of injustice, that would be so easy, so obvious and so tempting. 'Why me?' you could cry all day long. You could sink into rebellion, exhaust yourself with rage, lose yourself in hatred. But what would you gain from it? All the energy that you need to fight against the illness would be swallowed up by these violent destructive feelings."

"I can't help it! I feel so angry with the illness which is overcoming me. I'm full of hatred each time I think about my body, and imagine these diseased cells which are invading it all over. Powerless, I'm taken over by a feeling of injustice which completely destroys me."

"Don't let hatred enter your heart, it won't help you. It will rule you and will rob you of your freedom. To fight against the illness, you must mobilize all the positive forces, willpower, hope, courage and trust. Anger and hatred are destructive, they increase the harm, they sap the energy you need to be able to fight. Adopt a positive feeling in opposition to hatred, fight it with love which is the most powerful and the noblest weapon at your disposal, the love that surrounds you, the love you experience, the love of life. In the face of the strongest adversity, only an emotion which ennobles the dignity of a human being is powerful enough to win through."

"You are always telling me that misfortune makes you grow, but I don't feel as if I'm getting wiser or making progress, rather I think I'm stagnating, just staying still. When I was at school, I was actually learning something new in each lesson, and during the holidays I had interesting things to do, but here I'm not learning anything, I'm just waiting, sleeping, crying and waiting again..."

"Don't be misled, there are different ways of learning and growing. You told me the other evening that you felt you were cut off from life. Don't forget that life is to be found in immobility as well as in action, in suffering as much as in joy. There are no directions for use given to help face the tests of life. Each person must follow the path that leads to their own truth, to their own solution, groping and making mistakes, bumping into things, falling down and getting up again and again. Without moving, you are advancing on the way which will lead you to your innermost convictions, your deepest beliefs, your unique and true personality which will spring forth as a result of your efforts. Everyone must trace their own path towards their truth, that is the price of freedom, the price that must be paid for their choices which, alone, will hold in the face of the final step which they must take alone."

Part 2

14

So, once again, we are rushing to the hospital in the middle of the night. How many times have we done this in the last twelve months? It is true that it is almost a year since my leukaemia was diagnosed, on that black Tuesday in the first week of the summer holidays last year. My illness has completely shattered our lives, for all three of us. Mum has given up her work which she really enjoyed. Dad tries to be away from his work as little as possible, but, even so, he often finds himself having to leave a meeting or come back urgently from a business trip when I'm ill. My parents have worked out a plan which should allow them to save their time and energy as much as possible. For example, they never both come with me to the hospital when my temperature goes up in the night. Usually, it is Mum who takes me because Dad has to work the next day. They try to divide the time they spend with me at the hospital between them, as well as all the other things they have to do. While one of them sits with me, the other tries to catch up on lost sleep. Well, that's the theory. In practice it is much more chaotic and they never quite seem to get the balance right. When I'm in hospital, they spend as much time as possible with me, and avoid leaving me alone for too long. When we go back home, I'm usually still quite ill and I feel that Mum is overwhelmed by the responsibility of looking after me. When I'm in hospital, she is relieved of this task since the medical team takes care of everything. As soon as we go back home, however, Mum is there for me all the time, and normal housework stops. Dirty clothes pile up in the laundry room, next to the clean things waiting to be ironed. The flowers shrivel up in the garden because nobody waters them. Dirty dishes pile up in the sink. The house is a total mess. Mum sits in the middle of all this, too tired and overwhelmed to sort things out. Our cleaning lady doesn't come any more.

Any expenses which aren't absolutely vital have been cut from the family budget, because it's really hard to get by without Mum's wages. My illness is costing the whole family a great deal. However, I know that doesn't matter to my parents. The only thing that counts for them is my health, and they are there for me all the time. As well as looking after me, they constantly try to entertain me and make me laugh, fiercely determined to fill the home with a bit of lightheartedness and fun. As soon as I call Mum, or she hears me awake, she comes quickly into my room with a big smile on her beautiful tired face. I can see the infinite love that she feels for me in the way she looks at me, and I'm profoundly happy that she is there. I don't know how she manages to keep going.

~

The year that has just passed has been very difficult. The hardest thing is the constant distress eating away at me from the inside. Then there have been lots of visits to hospital. First of all, because of the regular sessions of "outpatient chemo" which brought me face to face with my illness each time. Then, because of various infections which followed, often meaning I had to stay in hospital for days at a time, even weeks. Each problem on its own was tolerable, I suppose, but they all added up to a situation that was unbearable, and made me really fed up with hospital. I had the feeling I was living in an endless nightmare with no way out. At the beginning of December, I got a terrible fright because my bones ached, and since I'd also lost weight, we immediately feared the worst. Thank heaven it was a false alarm. The results of the biopsy were good: they were probably growing pains, and I was still in remission. I was waiting for the day when they would finally say that I was cured, but that wouldn't happen for at least five years, according to Professor Granger. "But remission and cure are practically the same thing for you," he had said to reassure me. "Since you feel alright, the exact word doesn't matter to you, does it?"

"Not quite true," I said to myself in my heart of hearts, "contrary to what he seems to think, I can easily tell the difference between remission and cure. The first implies a constant threat hanging over my head, whereas the second means freedom and a future."

~

So, I learned to live with the fear of a relapse and in spite of everything I tried to have some good times, but never really succeeded. There were indeed periods of hope when I dared to imagine my future, but I also experienced times of great depression when the battle seemed to be lost already. This endless alternation between moments of high hope, which were almost euphoric, and moments of deep despair, was exhausting. I often thought of Angel's words encouraging me to fight the illness with fierce determination, choosing to be happy in spite of everything. Even though she is right that we can control the mood of our days to a certain extent, reality nevertheless catches us out, and I haven't often been able to rise above it.

The day that Professor Granger informed us that I had leukaemia, he had said, when talking about school, that the fellowship between young people is very great when one of them is in difficulties. That is true, but he forgot—or rather omitted—to mention that our friends' fellowship, for all that it's precious and important, doesn't really get through to us because we are somewhat apart. I mean, as far as I'm concerned anyway, that I'm completely wrapped up in my own problems and that I have great difficulty opening myself up to other people's concerns. Their heartaches, for instance, seem trivial and bore me. Their pleasure and pastimes appear superficial and I prefer to stay at home and read. I feel excluded from their lives, imprisoned in my own problems and fears, and light years away from their interests and preoccupations. I have really tried to reintegrate myself into normal life. Aware that by isolating myself, I was going to distance myself from them even more, I tried everything, but in vain. I'm a slave to my illness, not only physically, but even in my attitude to life. On top of that, the obsession with germs is pretty well ruining my life. As soon as one of the pupils in the class is ill, even if it is only a cold, I panic and stay away from them. Sometimes, I even stay at home to avoid catching an infection. With me, everything takes on alarming proportions. A minor cold can cause some complication followed by hospitalization and a course of antibiotics... that is why I'm obsessed by germs, and this makes me ultra-cautious, to the point of hysteria. I liked myself better the way I was before my illness. My former friends did so too, I think. I say "former", even if they are all there for me all the time, kind and loyal... but I'm not their friend any more, at least, not like before. Take Nicole, for example, whom I liked a lot, and whom I still like a lot: she has become very good friends with Alexandra with whom she goes horse riding. They have something in common and that has drawn them close together. It's like me with the sick children and teenagers: we have our cancer in common which binds us together more tightly than any sport or interest could do. We are fighting the same battle and we know exactly what the others are feeling, without any words being spoken. It is as if the strength of the bond grows with the importance of what is at stake, and our bond is fundamental since it is a matter of life and death!

~

Tonight, I'm more worried than on other occasions in the past when we've dashed frantically to hospital, because for some weeks I've noticed signs of a relapse, but I haven't said anything to anyone. I've been suffering from diffuse and intermittent aches and pains in my bones. What's more, I have noticed bruises. Every morning when I have my shower, I examine myself in the big mirror in the bathroom. From the moment I wake up, I'm weighed down and worried at the thought of finding a new blue/black mark on my body. Also, I've lost weight. I can hide all these symptoms from my parents, but not from myself. Now I know that aching bones can certainly be caused by growth, but equally by the large number of white corpuscles which cause tension in the bones. The bruises I found so alarming at the beginning of my illness were in fact local haemorrhages caused by my blood being too liquid. When you know all this, you can't act as if you didn't know, which is very annoying. Also, these last few weeks I've gorged myself in my efforts to put on weight, and I've slept a lot. But the tiredness remains, relentless and pitiless like a traitor within. Sometimes I'm so exhausted that I feel dizzy. All this has brought about a strange struggle between hope and terror within me. There are times when I tell myself that everyone has the right to lose a bit of weight, and to knock themselves, and that it's normal to have little aches and pains here and there. And what's more, we're getting to the end of the school year, and I have tried hard to do well in spite of all the lessons I have missed, and that's tiring. I go over all these arguments in my mind, tirelessly, and when after an intense effort of self-persuasion, I finally succeed in convincing myself, I'm overwhelmed with a feeling of relief. At those moments I'm uplifted and exuberant, and I feel like hugging everybody. But such moments are becoming more and more rare, and are being replaced by an undeniable evidence that chills and terrifies me: I'm having a relapse, cancerous cells have once again invaded my bone marrow and are pouring into my blood. And yet, despite these moments of great terror, I haven't said anything to anyone. In my confusion I thought that as long as reality isn't put into words, it doesn't exist. That is childish, for sure, but I suppose it is also human.

Mum is driving quickly, without speaking, she must think that I'm asleep. I realize that I haven't moved since the beginning of the journey. I'm incredibly tense and my jaws are clamped so tightly that they hurt. I suppose I've inherited that from Dad. I try to relax but I can't. I'm terrified of what is waiting for me. The biopsy first of all: I'm still as afraid of that as I was on the first day of my illness. The idea of the anaesthetic and being plunged into nothingness stresses me as much as ever. But that is nothing compared with the terrifying wait for the results. I'm sure that this time they will be bad. The truce is over. However, I have believed in it during the past year. Not always of course, but from time to time. I touch my hair which has grown again, and which is just as soft as it was before my illness, a symbol of my regained humanity. I couldn't bear to lose it in handfuls a second time. I no longer have the strength to put up with a new course of chemo. I say that, but I know it isn't true. In order to live I would do anything at all. We are approaching the emergency entrance to the university hospital. "My love," whispers Mum, "wake up, we've arrived."

15

At the hospital the events unfold according to a ritual that I know only too well. Temperature, blood pressure, blood samples, inserting the drip, paracetamol... I'm sick of it, will it ever end? The biopsy is arranged for the next morning for the first appointment. This sense of urgency fills me with panic and I sleep badly.

Professor Granger, who knows me well by now, notices immediately that I'm specially stressed this morning. I could swear he also knows why I'm more apprehensive about this biopsy than the others. The operation is short, and once I've woken up from the anaesthetic, I have to face the terrible, pitiless waiting. My parents have joined me in my room, which happens to be the same I occupied last year. We don't talk. The more imminent and important the danger is, the less people who love one another can communicate. At least that is how it is with us. Joy can be shared, for sure, but anguish separates people. Each one is alone with their own demons, face to face with themselves, confronting the limits of their endurance, of their capacity to stand up to it, calling on all their resources. In spite of my temperature, I'm in a state of high alert, as tense as a strung bow. Lying on my back, I'm so nervous that I stop breathing from time to time. As soon as I notice this, I try to breathe deeply which makes me hyperventilate, and this makes me dizzy. Time passes slowly, cruelly, it even seems to stop occasionally, as if trying to make me break down. Oh God, how I hate my life, how I hate my cancer!

Suddenly, I think of Angel, I think of our discussions and gradually I relax and a deep feeling of peace comes over me. "Calm down," I tell myself, "you can't change the course of things anyway." I breathe deeply and slowly several times, and eventually I look at my parents who haven't taken their eyes off me during all this time.

"I'm having a relapse," I say calmly. "Don't be pessimistic," Dad replies with alarm. I look at him and a feeling of enormous tenderness comes over me.

"I'm not pessimistic, Dad, I just know I'm having a relapse," I add gently. "Since when?" asks Mum, overwhelmed. I know she's been watching me in anguish every day since I became ill. "For a few weeks," I say. "Don't worry, don't blame yourself, Mum, a bit sooner or later, that won't change anything."

At that moment Professor Granger comes into the room. A single glance is enough, and we all have understood: I was right, I am in relapse. His expression shows this without doubt. In any case the message isn't difficult to get across, because, taking into account my catastrophic results, he certainly suspects that I must have known for quite some time. It's obvious that, unless I was completely cut off from my sensations, I'd have noticed the signs in my body. All four of us sit in the room bathed in summer sunshine and I have a curious impression of *déjà vu*, but not only "seen before", also "lived before" and "suffered before".

"Well," says Professor Granger, "the results give us no choice. After a few more tests we shall start a tough course of chemotherapy."

"A great programme," I say to myself bitterly, "better than holiday camp. It's worked out well, we're at the start of the summer holidays again!"

"If only we'd noticed this relapse," says Mum. It is hardly possible to understand what she is saying, as her voice is choked with sobs that she's trying to keep back. She who is usually so brave, so strong, is about to break down. It's true that my parents weren't expecting this staggering blow that has been dealt us. "Don't blame yourself," replies the doctor gently, "that wouldn't have made any difference. We are going to start immediately a new course of chemotherapy and your daughter will at last see the end of the tunnel." He is kind, he comforts her, no doubt he is trying to reassure me at the same time, but nobody is taken in by it, certainly not me.

~

Night has fallen and I have switched out the bedside lamp. I close my eyes and I'm immediately overcome by total panic: I've let the cancer spread in my body once more because I'm a coward! I was so scared of another biopsy, another course of chemo, of losing my hair again, that I let these diseased cells invade my blood without doing anything about it, and it's all my own fault! When I fell ill last year, it wasn't my fault, but this time I'm responsible for it. I bury my head in the pillow and am overcome with a fit of crying, and uncontrollable, ridiculous hiccups. I'm suffocating, I'm sweating and in a complete panic. At this moment the door opens as if by magic and Blanche's head appears. She is on duty tonight. Of course, I would have preferred it to be Sarah, but I have realized long ago now that my desires and wishes have no influence over the way things work out.

She sits on my bed and smiles at me kindly. I calm down a bit and we talk for a long time about one thing and another, nothing really important, but her presence is absolutely vital to me, and I know she realizes this. Some time later, her "beeper" starts to ring and she gets up. "I'll be back in a little while," she reassures me. In this hospital the team of carers always keep their promises, and this is comforting. I manage to relax a bit and close my eyes, holding Angel tightly next to my heart.

~

The next day I meet up with a group of friends at the evening meal. The youngest, Alexander, is seven. He is so shy that it makes him unsociable, except with Ingrid, his great friend.

Ingrid is fifteen, and she pampers him like a mother. She has got into the habit of playing board games with him for hours on end. We "big" ones usually spend our time talking about the illness, of course, and also about the ways of treating it.

After the meal, Ingrid, Benjamin and I go to listen to music in the common room. Ingrid is in low spirits. She is usually calm and patient, but now she's angry, almost at boiling point. "Why have we got this illness? Why us?" she keeps on saying. "What have we done to deserve it? What is this punishment that's been inflicted on us? And why, but why...?" At the same time as she gives way to her anger, she sinks further and further into deep despair. Benjamin and I look at each other with concern, not knowing what to say. Through listening to her rebelling against her illness, I too am seized by a feeling of total injustice. I feel uncomfortable, because I've often noticed Ingrid consoling Alexander, she always seems to find the right words. But Alexander has gone to bed and so now Ingrid can voice her dark thoughts. I myself don't have her ability to find comforting words. Angel and I have spoken about the injustice of illness, and her explanations have soothed me, but I don't feel that I'm ready to share them. It is difficult to convince someone when the feelings of rebellion and despair are so immense. I feel absolutely useless and Ingrid's distress flows towards me like red-hot lava, engulfing me completely. "There must be *some* reason..." suggests Benjamin, hoping to comfort her. "What reason?" asks Ingrid, and her question sounds like the crack of a whip. "I don't know, Ingrid, I don't know either," Benjamin answers wearily. That evening our conversation does us no good at all, and we leave one another more dejected and alone than if we had spent the evening by ourselves in our rooms.

It takes a long time to get to sleep, going over these questions in my mind and looking vainly for answers. Although Ingrid's despair has overwhelmed me, giving me back my own dejection and increasing it, I notice nonetheless that it's good to be able to say everything to one another. Among ourselves we have no need to play games, to be strong all the time, to smile when we want to cry or shout out our feelings of revolt. When we're with our parents, we constantly put on a happy face so as not to upset them even more, or else, when that is too hard, we say nothing. Curiously, we feel guilty about being ill, guilty for making them suffer, and we are ready to try any ways and means to protect them. Suddenly, I realize there is another reason for our behaviour. Through a game of mirrors, we rise above our reality. On the edge of the abyss, we smile bravely, and the image which is reflected in our parents' eyes comforts us and is transformed into a real force which helps us to go on.

16

Some days later, I go to the common room in the hope of meeting some friends. I'm bored and I want to talk to somebody. James and Stephen are there, watching a video. I don't know them very well, but we have already played cards together a few days ago. I watch the screen without feeling much interest in the film which seems violent and stupid. I'm getting ready to leave when James asks me to wait a bit. "The film is almost finished, we can go and drink a coke on the terrace, if you like."

"Okay," I reply, picking up a magazine lying around on the table. Their film is over at last. We go down and sit on the terrace which is crowded with patients and visitors. Our conversation quickly becomes serious, for we are all obsessed with the idea of death.

"What's it like when you die?" asks Stephen. He is younger than us and must imagine because of this that we know more about it than he does. This, however, is not the case.

"I suppose it hurts," I answer.

"I asked Fiona the other evening," James says. "She's been on duty this week. It seems that some boy just died in the isolation ward. He was waiting for a transplant, that's why we've never seen him. Fiona assured me he didn't suffer, but she didn't want to tell me any more about it. I've noticed that the nurses are willing to talk about anything except death. Perhaps they're as frightened of it as we are."

"All the same, they're adults," I reply, "they ought to be more clued up than us. What's more they are not ill. I rather think they don't want to upset us."

"But we're upset anyway," contradicts James, "even if nobody talks to us about it. We keep going over these questions in our own minds, that's far worse than being able to discuss it with someone."

"What worries me is not knowing where I'll go when I'm dead," adds Stephen, thoughtfully.

"Perhaps you won't go anywhere, you'll be dead, that's all," retorts James.

"You mean I'll have to stay in a coffin forever?" asks Stephen, anxious.

"Your body will be in a coffin, but maybe you'll go to heaven," I add, hoping to comfort him.

Stephen asks with curiosity:

"Will I turn into an angel and fly away to paradise?"

James answers, laughing:

"I don't know if you're good enough to be an angel, you don't look much like it!"

"All the same, you don't think he'll go to hell!" I say to James, in a joking tone.

And he replies:

"These stories of heaven and hell seem stupid to me. I wanted to stop going to Sunday School because of that, but my parents got angry and made me go back. I think quite simply that when you are dead, you are dead—end of story!"

"I think I believe in heaven," I explain, "or if you don't like that word, in a better world that we go to when we die."

"That's what Mum says too," adds Stephen eagerly, relieved that someone shares his mum's view.

James retorts in a harsh tone:

"Perhaps, but nobody really knows. Priests don't either, they haven't been there. It's just an idea."

"Okay," I admit, "but it's more reassuring than thinking that you just stop existing."

But James remains inflexible:

"As you say, it's more reassuring, but that doesn't mean it has to be true. It simply makes you feel better believing in it."

I add, slightly discouraged:

"It's a shame nobody has come back from the dead. They could tell us about it."

We go on a bit longer with our discussion which gets us nowhere. I realize that we're all at the same point. We're all asking the same questions, but nobody has an answer, only ideas, theories, wishing for a better world, or obstinately refusing to believe in it. I think about my conversations with Angel, about the consciousness which flies away like a butterfly towards its new destiny. I want to talk to the others about it, but the idea is still too fragile in my mind to put up with their cries of disbelief. And how can I tell them that it's my doll who has told me all these wonderful things? I'd like to share my thoughts with them, because I think they'd be comforted by them, but at the same time, I'm aware that each one of us must find their own path to their truth. What is becoming a conviction for me, even if it is still vulnerable, would maybe not persuade them.

The terrace has emptied, the visitors have left, and the patients have gone back to their rooms. "It's time for dinner," I say regretfully. "We'd better go."

~

A week has gone by since the start of the chemo. When Professor Granger talked about a "tough chemotherapy" he wasn't mistaken in his choice of adjective. This chemo is a thousand times worse than last year's. My body is completely devastated by the violence of the medication. I can feel the poison going along every vein, every artery, penetrating into every corner of my body, destroying everything as it goes. I'm breaking down, gasping for breath, vomiting my guts out, spitting out with all my strength and hatred this venom that's killing me from the inside. They are now long gone, the innocent days when I thought that the chemo was certain to cure me. Last year, though it made me sick, I saw it as an ally. Today I hate it as a murderous enemy which I want to tear to shreds with my teeth. My fury is equal to the violence of its side-effects. I'm no longer the docile patient, following the medical staff's instructions to the letter. Today I'm the rebellious patient, let down by medicine, betrayed by the doctors' promises, all alone on a trail across the desert, which could just as easily lead to an oasis as it could to death hidden behind the sand-dunes burning... with fever. Everything is jostling in my head and I think I must be delirious.

17

My favourite doll is lying on my pillow, waiting for me, and as soon as the nurse has turned out the lights, I'm able to talk to her.

"Last night I had a dream and then something strange happened to me."

"Do you want to tell me about it?"

"Yes, but I can't remember it all. In my dream I was on a boat with my parents in the middle of a storm. It was dark but the moon was shining on the water with a silvery light. The sea was wild and huge waves were breaking on the deck of the boat which was pitching dangerously. I was fascinated and at the same time frightened by the fury of the waves and the roaring of the storm. Lots of people were bustling around on the boat and running all over the place. I didn't move, I couldn't take my eyes off this wonderful spectacle and each new wave that broke on the deck drenched me. I could feel the cold going through my wet clothes, and yet I wasn't ready to leave my place and stop looking at this wild storm. Suddenly, I found myself on an island plunged in darkness, all alone, wet through and trembling with cold. I knew my parents weren't there anymore and someone that I couldn't see was telling me to go to a house at the end of the road, beside a church. I panicked because I'm afraid of the dark, I can never find the places I'm trying to get to, and what's more, I was sure I would be attacked on the way. But the only thing I could do was to obey, so I set off. Unexpectedly the road was lit and much shorter than I thought, and soon I noticed a pretty little church at the end. It was a nice surprise to find my journey was so simple, and I was quite proud of myself for finding the place so easily and not to have lost my way. Next to the church was a big house and suddenly, I found myself inside it, in a warm and friendly atmosphere. Greatly relieved,

I took off my soaking clothes which I threw carelessly onto the floor, and someone offered me a white night gown made of light floaty material. I put it on at once and slipped into a soft warm bed. I sank down in delight into the squashy soft pillows and closed my eyes giving a sigh of pleasure.

"At that moment, I opened my eyes and looked across my hospital room here in the half-light, and saw my grandmother come into view at the foot of my bed. Although she has been dead for some time, it seemed quite natural for her to be there; I was definitely not surprised to see her. Her silhouette stood out vaguely against the back of my room, lit up by the pale moonlight coming in through the window. We began to talk. I was half asleep and don't remember the conversation very well, but I know it was about my illness and the fact that I was wrong to worry about it so much. My grandmother explained that everything would be all right for me, no matter what the outcome of my leukaemia was. All that she said to me seemed obvious as if I had always known it. When I woke up the next morning, I felt comforted and happy in a way that I haven't been since I fell ill."

"When you have visions like this, you have to take them seriously."

"So, you think it's true?"

"Are you asking me if I believe what you say?"

"No, I suppose you trust me not to tell lies. No, I'm asking if you believe it's true that I saw my grandmother."

"What do you mean by 'true'?"

"You seem to be deliberately misunderstanding me! I'm asking if you think it's possible that my grandmother spoke to me."

"Why do you ask *me* this question? It's you that it happened to, so you know better than anyone what took place."

"I know I saw my grandmother but I don't know if I can believe it."

"Do you mean that you doubt the real presence of your grandmother?"

"Yes, I don't know if it was just my imagination, or maybe my desire, that brought about this encounter with her."

"What proof do you need to believe in it, or rather to accept it?"

"I don't know. I just wonder if people who are dead can come and talk to us in the night."

"It isn't really a question of true or false, real or imaginary. The real value of your vision lies in what it means to you. Take it to be a sign, like a present given specially to you and you alone. A sign of this kind is by its nature personal, intimate and infinitely precious. It is meaningful only to you. Measure the truth of it by the impact that is has upon you, by the good it does you, by the consolation that it brings, by the answers it offers you. Only you can give it its meaning and its true dimension, for it belongs to you alone."

"But how is it possible that I talked with my grandmother who is dead?"

"Do you remember the game we invented which transported us into the magic world of the absolute being? Do you remember the idea of the game?"

"Yes, I can remember."

"In this encounter in the night you will have seen a different facet of your grandma. When someone is in turmoil and great trouble, this other dimension is revealed by an act of consolation and love. The answers offered are equal to the intensity of the distress. Nobody is ever left alone, provided, of course, they have the necessary trust to recognize the signs."

"You seem to be able to understand what my grandmother intended, perhaps that's because she knitted you..."

~

The next evening I'm lying in my bed and I feel sad. I'm obsessed with the idea of my death, whether it will be near or a long way off. I would so much like to get better, to leave the hospital and go home, but I have ended up realizing that my desires don't count for much in this stream of life that's drawing me towards an uncertain future. Night has fallen and I'm lying on my back. I've been looking up at the ceiling for quite a long time. The hospital room, lit only by the bedside lamp, is half in darkness. Everything is quiet, Mum is asleep in the armchair beside me. Her hair is greasy; because of me she hasn't had time to wash it. Suddenly, I feel calm, almost happy. At certain moments I withdraw into my suffering and become one with it. I'm totally immersed in myself and the world around doesn't interest me anymore. In fact, I feel separate from it. I suppose it's tiredness bringing on this feeling. Or maybe the idea of death? Perhaps it is really quite near, although I see it so far off in spite of my illness? Thoughts keep on coming of their own accord into my mind and draw me towards states of consciousness which are closer to intuition than reflection. I tell myself, or rather something deep inside tells me, that the two outcomes, being cured or dying, are perhaps equally good. If I could get better, obviously I would continue my life gratefully and with immense relief. But this isn't guaranteed. With this thought I feel myself swinging between a state of mind which forces me to fight and to put up with anything in the hope of a better future, and a more advanced stage that invites me, not to resignation, but to acceptance. These ideas must come from my conversations with Angel, my very special doll who tells me magic stories in the evening just before I go to sleep.

18

I've had a horrible and exhausting day, but actually no more horrible or exhausting than those before. The carers continue to bludgeon my body with their aggressive medication. When I think of that, I see them as enemies, torturers, when I should really think of them as allies or perhaps even saviours. But at this moment it's impossible to be grateful for the efforts they're making on my behalf. I can feel all the violence of the treatment attacking my body from the inside. I feel as if they're poisoning me bit by bit by injecting this filthy stuff into me every day. I certainly don't have a grudge against Professor Granger, or the nurses who I really like. No, I'm angry with adults, with the entire medical profession which is incapable of anything better than poisoning us, the patients, with their chemo which doesn't only eradicate the cells that are affected — again, in my case it hasn't even been able to do that! — but kills us slowly by destroying our healthy cells as well. Leukaemia is more treacherous than any other form of cancer because it has no precise location. It lodges in the bones as well as in the blood circulating around the whole body. A tumour which grows on an organ, on the liver for instance, can be visualized mentally, you can draw a line around it and then say that the rest of the body is healthy. For those of us with leukaemia, that's impossible because the enemy is lurking everywhere. Like a ghost, it conceals itself cowardly in the blood and overwhelms us completely. Apart from the disastrous effects of the chemo, leukaemia isn't painful. There again, it is treacherous. The immense suffering it inflicts upon us isn't so much physical as psychological, nourished by exhaustion, anguish about the future and the fear of dying.

My physical problems plunge me into a terrible contradiction regarding my body. On the one hand I'm totally bound to it, to such a degree that I still cannot imagine that I could be separated from it. On the other hand, I hate it. And this hatred is terrible, total, and infinitely sad. My body has betrayed me, that's for sure. What's worse, it is depriving me of my future, of my life, perhaps. The immense confusion I'm prey to makes me dizzy. I try with all the strength of my being to imagine myself without my body, to conceive of what I should become after my death— the death of my body—but I cannot manage it.

The days follow one after another and they are all alike. Time grinds on slowly, and the chemo becomes harder and harder to bear. I'm still suffering from nausea and each day I get more and more exhausted. Today I have spent the whole time lying in bed with my parents around me. Some of my friends have called in to say hello, but they didn't stay because there is an unspoken agreement, we respect the desire of those who want to rest in their rooms.

~

For some days I've spent the best part of my time in bed, prey to a fathomless exhaustion, mingled with a crucifying boredom. I say "crucifying" because it's very different from the ordinary boredom that every girl experiences. You can be bored at home in the holidays when you have nothing to do. You can be annoyed in the company of people who have nothing interesting to say. You can be bored to death by a maths lesson when you cannot understand it at all, but that has *nothing* to do with the tedium I'm talking about. This tedium, which is near disgust, is deadly, because it kills the desire to live, it excludes life. Nothing has any importance anymore, and there is not a single project on the horizon. Everything is hopeless and absurd. The profound feeling of tedium, the absence of any purpose, the denial of life is mixed up with my exhaustion. At the same time, it's due to my physical inability to get up and do things, and also to the psychological depression which prevents me from taking any interest in the world around me. So, being unable to act, I've been in a permanent state of waiting since the day my illness was diagnosed. I have waited for visits from doctors, for the results of tests, for the chemo to take effect, for the treatment to work. I have waited for a cure, and today I'm waiting for death. All my life I shall have waited... in vain. That is where my parents' love becomes a constraint. I feel that soon I shan't have the strength to struggle, to suffer or to hope. I know the final proof of love they'll have to find the strength to give me will be to let me go. But nobody's ready for that yet, not them, not me. However, I feel that I am approaching the end of the road. Tedium and despair are paralysing me. All those seconds, minutes, hours, days are passing without bringing a solution, and my body is slowly and inevitably disintegrating...

~

The chemo is finished, but my ordeal isn't over yet as I'm utterly exhausted, drained of all my energy. It wasn't simply through cowardice that I rejected the evidence of my relapse. It was something stronger than cowardice, a powerful presentiment of something that would be very hard to bear. However, I didn't expect what I'm now living through. I know that Professor Granger wants to give me every chance, but I wonder if he isn't going to kill me with this violent chemo.

At the start of my illness, I was in shock, that's for sure, stressed and bewildered at the same time, but nonetheless I kept hoping, which is a powerful tool for getting along the twisty path of life. I believed in the curative power of chemo. I trusted the omnipotence, or at least the vast expertise, of the medical team. I was somehow convinced that my suffering would be rewarded by my complete recovery. It's true that the normal course of my life had been seriously upset by the leukaemia. In that sense there had already been a significant deviation in the course of my life, but I remained confident: this was only to be a painful parenthesis in my existence, a time of trial through which one grows as a person, as Professor Granger had so nicely predicted. In spite of being dealt this blow of fate, I felt I had a future, *my* future. Today everything is different, chaotic, and nothing is certain. I have realized sadly that it isn't enough to be a good patient in order to get better, like being a good pupil to do well in my exams. It isn't enough, either, to pray to God to be cured. It's much more complicated than that. Contrary to what I'd imagined, courage by itself, along with chemo, of course, doesn't get rid of cancerous cells. The logic of all this escapes me completely and I feel like a little boat bobbing around on a rough sea in a violent storm. My chances of treading once more on land seem to be minimal. I realize this quite clearly. What's more, the painful, throbbing questions that I ask myself about merit and blame remain unanswered, unless I believe what Angel says, which helps me make some sense of my doubts, and which is the only defence against the pit of despair. Yes, I'm ready to follow her advice when she suggests quite simply trusting and waiting until the last piece of the puzzle of life is fitted in harmoniously and naturally when the time is right.

19

Today, Luke, a medical student, is on duty on our ward. He is so handsome that it almost hurts me to look at him. I wonder what he is doing here in this hospital. I mean he could have been an actor; he is so good-looking with his olive complexion and his dark brown velvety eyes. My parents, who know my tastes, have always teased me saying I'm sure to marry a Mediterranean type, and that always made me laugh. Today it makes me cry for I'm afraid that I'll never marry anyone. Luke, who has just finished his round, has come to sit on my bed. I'm troubled by his presence. I feel myself blush and that annoys me because I wonder what he will think. He only stays for a little while, because he usually says goodnight to all the young people on our floor and there are a lot of us. However, rather than talking about unimportant subjects such as my temperature graph or some medication which has just been changed, I'd prefer to talk to him about what is really bothering me. I start dreaming up a conversation that would hurt me and comfort me at the same time. I start to talk about the possibility of my death. I expect him to be straightforward but now when he speaks, I'm struck dumb by his honesty. Struck dumb and frightened at the same time. To my question about my chances of survival, he replies: "Not very good." He avoids saying "not good" because he wants to leave a little door open for hope, but we both know that it's only out of compassion that he has added "very". I wanted the truth and I've got it, like a punch in the stomach. It takes my breath away. However, though deep down I know this truth, I shall never get used to it. When I say "never", that implies a future which maybe I no longer have. He looks deep into my eyes and it makes my heart skip a beat. Then he sits closer to me and takes my hand in his. It is so sweet and tender that, for the moment, I forget that he's trying to console me for my sad fate, and his intention isn't to seduce me. But if I weren't ill, he would not need to console me, and anyway I wouldn't have met him, because I would never have had anything to do with paediatric oncology. We stay like this for a long time, in silence, while the sky slowly darkens. It is a moment of real happiness even if it is tinged with sadness. Never since the day I was told of my leukaemia have I been happy without feeling sad at the same time, even if I have done all I could to snatch back a bit of ground from the illness, to let life have the upper hand against all the odds, as Angel had advised me to do. "How much time do you give me?" It is with these terrible words that I break the silence. "If it was up to me, I'd give you all the time in the world." I really like his answer, it is beautiful and elusive as well, of course. He gives me a big smile and I lose myself in the depths of his gaze. Suddenly, at this precise instant, I realize what I'm going to lose, or never experience, which amounts to the same thing. I could have become a woman and been loved by a Luke or, who knows, by Luke himself... There, it is not a punch in the stomach now, more a knife stuck right into my heart. I start to sob so violently that it chokes me. Luke is distraught. "Don't cry, please," he says, abashed. He doesn't know what else to say. He can't lie, and that's why I think so highly of him, but apart from an untruth, there is really nothing to be said, nothing to be done—except to take me into his arms and cuddle me gently until my sobs die down. I know he won't do that. He pats my hand and smiles at me tenderly. He feels bad for me. I tell myself that he'll be a good doctor because he'll love his patients—all of them, the boys as much as the girls, the unattractive ones as much as the good-looking ones.

I know he'll feel a genuine compassion for everyone, without preference and without exception. That makes me sad all the same, for I would have liked him to empathise only with me, and I don't want anyone else to be lost as I am in the depths of his gaze, but I'm aware that after me he will take care of other girls. The idea of this grieves me so much that I give way to another outburst of crying. He moves a little closer to me and starts to stroke my head. I cry for a long time, but I know he won't leave me. We remain silent, for there is nothing more to say. Night has now fallen completely and darkness surrounds us. He continues stroking my head at regular intervals, almost mechanically, while we are both lost in our thoughts, thoughts which are of course different and yet similar, no doubt. For him it is the powerlessness of the doctor confronted by illness and the fury that this causes him, which is tormenting him; for me it is the terror of what is waiting for me that makes my blood run cold. And yet I feel good in his presence, protected, safe, knowing that he is so near in the night which silences all the daytime noises. We are alone, isolated from the rest of the world, united in one silence charged with emotion and sadness. My sobs become less frequent and I give myself up to sleep, for I know that Luke won't leave me. I dream so vividly of his presence and our conversation that I no longer know whether they are real or not. The next day when I wake up, he is no longer there.

20

The last few days have gone by with the relentless hospital routine where treatment and empty time follow each other so predictably and boringly. My exhaustion gives me a short break. I feel a bit better. I've spent part of the day with my father who has been reading the newspapers, sitting next to my bed. My world has shrunk considerably, and I'm short of subjects to talk about. Before my illness, I used to talk to my parents all the time. I told them stories about school, I negotiated permission for outings with friends, I asked them questions about my homework. Today, I'm turned in upon myself, and I don't talk much. However much my mind is overflowing with questions, I keep them to myself. After my father has left, I spend a long time with my friends playing cards. Finally, I find myself alone with Ingrid and we start to talk.

"Do you remember our discussion with Benjamin when you were so indignant with being ill? Do you feel any better?" I ask her.

"No, I feel just as bad, but I don't talk about it anymore. The same questions keep on coming back into my mind and I go round in circles, it's like an obsession. I keep wondering why I fell ill, what I did to deserve it. Sometimes I feel it's my fault, as if I'd done something wrong that triggered the cancer. At other times I feel I'm the victim of such a huge injustice that I've got a grudge against the whole world."

"I never felt I was to blame for having leukaemia, but I feel responsible for my relapse. I knew quite well that I had become ill again, but I refused to admit it. I didn't say anything to anyone."

"I can understand that. You didn't want to start the chemo again, but you didn't get away with it. But why has this happened to us?"

"Maybe our systems have just got out of balance for no special reason. It happened to us just as it might have happened to anyone."

Ingrid answers outraged:

"That's even worse! What bad luck! No, I can't get it out of my head that it's a punishment."

"What dreadful thing could you have done to deserve such an awful illness? Stop asking yourself these questions. I've been through all that myself, but it's no use. I think we've got to accept that we can't understand why we're ill and we should gather up all our strength to fight the illness. Rather than getting indignant, I try to find some sense in what's happening to me."

"You make me laugh! What sense could there be in this rotten illness?"

"It seems that it could make us grow as people."

"I'm not interested in growing. All I want is to get better."

"But it's true that I've learnt a lot of things since I've been ill. I'll never be the same person again. If I get better one day, I think that life will seem easy. The little problems that bothered me before will seem nothing to me, I'm sure I'll enjoy every moment of life. Simply waking up in the morning without being overwhelmed with the worry of my illness will be wonderful. My joy at being cured will probably die down in time, but I'm sure that I'll never forget all that leukaemia has taught me."

"Do you think the illness makes us better people?"

"I don't know, but it certainly changes us. It makes us realize that life is precious because of its fragility, because it isn't infinite. Before our illness we knew we'd die one day, of course, but it was so far away that it didn't seem real. Today we're aware that it isn't necessarily normal for life to keep going on steadily, for days to follow one after the other peacefully, and for us to see the sun rise each day for years on end. For us, nothing is certain anymore, nothing is guaranteed and in spite of our problems, that gives life a very special flavour. In this sense, the illness teaches us a real lesson, and makes us grow up faster than our friends outside. Being aware of the intrinsic value of life at the very moment when it may be taken from us... Do you realize...? What a paradox, and, at the same time, what a lesson!"

"It's true that we are more mature than our friends."

"More mature, perhaps, but above all, different. During the year I was in remission, it became clear to me that I no longer had the same interests and concerns as my friends, or, above all, the same dreams. All the time I was out of phase with them, as if I were in a different world."

"Yes, I've felt like that too. People who are healthy irritate me. On one hand I envy them a lot for not having my problems; on the other hand, I find them selfish and insensitive. I get the impression they don't understand me. I prefer the company of the patients here, at least we are all in the same boat. I feel at my best when I look after Alexander. When I comfort him and tell him everything will be all right, I almost believe it myself. By comforting him, I feel useful and less vulnerable, as if I'd taken charge of events."

"I admire you. I would never have your patience. But it's true that it's good to talk to someone. I talk to my doll."

Ingrid exclaims laughing:

"Aren't you rather old to be talking to dolls?"

"Probably, but this is a special doll, she's called Angel... Do you think about death yourself?"

"Of course, everybody here thinks about it. Above all I'm afraid of suffering."

"It seems that it doesn't hurt when you die."

"What do you know about it?"

"Fiona told James the other night."

"You know the nurses don't know everything. What's more they don't tell you all they know. I wonder where you go when you die..."

"James thinks that you don't go anywhere, that you just cease to exist: end of story!"

Ingrid smiles:

"I like the expression, but I don't like the idea. I rather think that you go to heaven, or let's say I make myself believe it."

"Maybe it is true, even if it makes us feel better believing in it, it could still be true. I imagine a better world where we would be happier than here, with no illness, no problems and no worries."

"How would we get into your better world?"

"We would fly, like butterflies, leaving our bodies behind."

"Do you really think it's possible? And how would you leave your body, at what moment?"

"In the same moment you die."

"Nobody's ever seen anyone leaving their body and flying away. How can you believe such a thing?"

"I don't know how it could work in practice, but I believe it's possible. Lots of things happen without us being able to see them."

"What, for example?"

"I haven't got an example, but I'm thinking of *The Little Prince* where it says that 'the essential is invisible'."

"That's just literature."

"Perhaps, but we can imagine that there is a world that we can't see, a world parallel to ours."

"And how do you imagine it?"

"Beautiful and peaceful. The people would all be joyful and would never quarrel. You would only do there what you want to do, like bathing in a lake or reading books."

"You really think there would be books there? And lakes? In fact, you are imagining a world like ours, but more beautiful and without problems."

"Why not?"

"That seems to me a bit simplistic. All we need now is the good Lord sitting on a cloud."

"Don't make fun. You know things happen to me that I wouldn't have believed possible. The other night my grandma came to see me."

Ingrid asks incredulously:

"Didn't you tell me that she was dead?"

"She is. Even so, she came to see me."

"You must have been dreaming."

"No, I wasn't dreaming, I was dozing, it's true, but I wasn't asleep."

"You aren't just going a bit mad?"

I defend myself laughing:

"No, I'm not mad! Angel was right. You have to know how to recognize the signs, but you must also know how to keep them to yourself."

"What do you mean by 'sign'?"

"A sign is when something appears to help people in difficulty. Signs are personal and can only be understood by the person that gets them. That's why I was wrong to talk to you about it. You're not involved, so you think I'm mad. It's normal."

"You really are starting to get me worried."

"Forget what I said. Do you believe in God?"

"At the beginning of my illness, I prayed a lot. I promised God I'd become a very good and kind person, if He would cure me. But as far as I can see, it hasn't worked. Either I didn't pray hard enough, or He doesn't exist."

"I'm not sure it works like that. I think it's much more complicated. I pray too, but mostly in order to feel less alone."

21

The next day I'm feeling a bit better and I leave my room to go to the communal dining room. As I turn at the end of the corridor, I find myself face to face with Stephen. He almost knocked me over and he is quite out of breath.

"Come on, come and see," he shouts excitedly. "What's the matter with him now?" I wonder. Disasters happen to Stephen all the time. This time, by contrast, he not only seems excited, but joyful as well. "Don't you know what's happened to James?" he shouts, "He's been to heaven!"

"What!" I feel my legs turn weak. I really like James; I don't want him to die. Not him! Not another one! And why does this death make Stephen so joyful? Has he gone mad? "Is he dead?" I ask, overwhelmed. "Oh no, he just went to heaven, then came back," answers Stephen.

If I didn't have Angel, I would tell myself that too much chemo is harmful to the brain, and that poor Stephen is out of his mind. But it so happens that I have a doll called Angel who talks to me in the evenings about strange and fascinating things, so Stephen's words remind me of something... "Calm down, Stephen," I say, "take a deep breath and tell me!"

"James died last night, you know, because of complications to do with his transplant. He'd had it for good with cardiac arrest and everything. I thought to myself, 'that's another mate gone and that brings the rest of us nearer to the grave', because of the 'inauspicious psychosomatic effect of the death of a companion suffering from the same illness', as they say. And then what do I hear? That James is lying in bed, white as a sheet, with his eyes shining. It seems that he keeps repeating: 'I've seen God, my grandmother, my cousin, my uncles and some wonderful horses. I want to return there, who made me come back?'"

"That reminds me of something," I say. "I'm going to see him."

All James's family is gathered around his bed. Even so, I put my head round the door of his room, and he winks at me in a knowing way that means, "I wish they would hurry up and leave, I want to talk to you", but they keep hanging on. I go back several times to his room. They are still there at the end of the afternoon, and in the evening, Agnes doesn't allow me to go and see him.

~

I didn't get permission to see James until three days later. It's true that he isn't the same any more. His face is peaceful, his eyes are shining. He's very pale and also very weak. I feel afraid of seeing him so ill, and yet an incredible power shines out of him, strong and new. It seems to reveal itself through his eyes. James has never been so radiant and full of comfort. Just seeing him, I feel better.

I ask him:

"What happened? It seems you nearly died?"

James answers with a big smile:

"I didn't *nearly* die, I did die! I was dead, Dr Tomala told me. I was in cardiac arrest for several minutes. I feel angry with him for having brought me round. I don't think I'll ever forgive him."

"Tell me about it," I say, while sitting on his bed.

"You'll never believe me; I'd rather not say anything at all..."

"I think I'll understand," I reassure him with a smile. "Thanks to Angel, I think I'll understand."

"Who's Angel?"

"It's my angel, well, an angel, it's my doll who is called Angel. Anyway, tell me!"

He is starting to talk when the door of the room opens noisily. His mother comes in, her arms full of parcels. "Hello, kids," she says cheerfully. "How are you today? I've made a cake," she says to James, "that one with walnuts that you like so much, you know. And I also brought you some comics. Oh, I forgot, I've also brought you a dish of apricot purée for tea."

"They do feed us here, Mum," replies James with a smile, "there's no need to make cakes for me. Anyway, I'm not hungry."

"That's exactly why I'm bringing you the things you like, to build up your strength. Your father will be here in a minute, he's just buying you some magazines at the kiosk down below." I realize regretfully that James's parents are settling for the afternoon, and I know from experience that in the evening, I shan't be allowed to come back, because the nurses check up rigorously on our sleep. The carers are very kind, it's true, but they are strict; all the same, we aren't in our own homes here. James smiles at me and says quietly while his mother puts the cake on the table at the end of the room: "There's no way we can talk in peace in this hospital! Tonight, I'll write you a letter to tell you what happened to me. I'll ask Blanche to give it to you. Tomorrow if you like, we'll talk about it."

"Okay," I reply, feeling less disappointed, and I go out of his room.

22

At about ten o'clock the door opens quietly and Blanche's head appears. "Aren't you asleep?" she asks me. "No, I was waiting for you to bring James's letter."

"Of course," she says, "here it is. But don't read it tonight, it's too late, you must go to sleep."

"Don't worry, I'll read it tomorrow."

As soon as the door closes, I quickly immerse myself in reading James's letter which consists of many sheets of paper.

I'm starting to feel really very ill. It is about 11 pm and the hospital is in silence. I'm aware that my body is violently rejecting the bone marrow transplant. They have increased the dose of the anti-rejection medication, but in spite of that, I feel worse and worse, my body aches, I feel sick and I have a very bad headache. I feel my desire to live and my energy escape slowly. However, I tell myself that if I give up, I shall die. I know that I must struggle to stay alive. To fight in my head, I mean, still to have the desire to live, but I realize that I no longer have the strength to do it. What's the good, I ask myself, it's finished. I'm aware that if I close my eyes, I shall never open them again. And I close them deliberately. I would have liked my parents to be there to be able to hug them for the last time, but they left at about nine o'clock, and so I prepare myself to die alone.

Suddenly, I feel that I'm leaving my body. Like a feather, I rise up into the air. I float gently towards the ceiling where I stay without moving. From this position, I look down and see a body stretched out on the bed beneath me. It is very curious: I don't know who this boy is, with his eyes closed, pale and still. He looks very ill. Or perhaps he is dead? Suddenly, I realize that it is me. I have never seen myself from the outside. When I look at myself in the mirror or on a photo, it doesn't give the same impression at all. There I see myself as a whole, as if it were another person, but there is no doubt that it is really me. This discovery doesn't frighten me, the most it does is to astonish me. I feel as if I'm in a totally safe place while my body is dying. I look at this livid body, this face contorted with pain, and I feel completely detached, without sadness or regret at having abandoned it. The pain has disappeared, and I notice that I have immediately lost all interest in my physical life. I realize that the frontier between life and death is only a strange illusion of our mind. It is horrifying and frightening seen from the point of view of living people, and yet it becomes totally insignificant when observed from the other side. My first impression is one of complete surprise. How is it possible that I exist in such a pleasant way, that I can observe and think, although I'm dead and without a body?

At that moment Agnes, who is on duty that night, comes into my room. When she sees me, she understands the situation at once and calls for help. Immediately, she bends over me and does mouth to mouth resuscitation, like you see in the films. While she is busy with my body, I look at the back of her neck. Curiously I can see each hair as well as its follicle on Agnes' head. I know exactly how many hairs she has and that delights me. I change my perspective and I see that she is wearing shiny nylon tights. Every reflection and sparkle stand out with a dazzling clarity, and again I know exactly how many sparkles there are. I begin to inspect the room, and I notice that I can see it all at the same time. I look at the top of the ceiling lamp, and at the underneath of my bed, at the same time. I can see the objects in front and behind me, simultaneously. I'm enjoying an all-round detailed vision. I look at my body again without understanding all this fuss around it, because at this stage other nurses and the duty doctor have joined Agnes. "Blanche, go round the other side," shouts the doctor, speaking to Agnes. I can feel Agnes' surprise, tinged with annoyance, and, at the same time, the doctor's embarrassment as he has just realized that in his haste, he has mistaken her name. He starts a cardiac massage counting out loud. Another nurse rushes into my room pushing an apparatus on a small trolley, and they immediately place electrodes on my bare chest. The doctor gives instructions and someone starts up the machine. My body is raised several centimetres above the bed, and I can hear a funny noise, like bones cracking. There is a great feeling of agitation in the room, and I wish it would all stop. "Leave my body alone!" I say loudly. "Stop working so hard on my body, can't you see that I'm not there anymore?" But they seem not to realize, and nobody listens to me, they are so preoccupied with this poor envelope of empty grey flesh which really doesn't deserve all this attention.

They are talking to one another, the doctor issues brief instructions, the nurses call out the numbers that they read on the machine. I can hear what they are saying, but not in a hearing manner. In fact, I cannot really hear because I have no ears which could transmit sounds to my brain, and what is more, I no longer have a brain. It is something quite different that I discover with astonishment and delight. An omniscience which I cannot explain enables me to know all the thoughts and emotions of the people present in the room. I know what they are thinking, exactly what they are thinking, without any possible doubt. I'm aware of the words a fraction of a second before they are spoken. At this moment I'm beside a nurse who is working the machine, and I catch hold of her arm to stop her starting it up again. To my great surprise my hand goes straight through her arm. I cannot understand what is happening, I don't feel any contact with her arm which I'm trying to grip. At this moment I notice that I haven't really got any hands, but I feel as if I have. I'm very much aware of my body, it is whole and I feel complete; my whole person is there, even though it isn't. It is very curious. I have the impression that I'm pure consciousness equipped with a fluid immaterial body with a blurred outline. So, I cannot take hold of the nurse, and she presses the button again, and my body jerks up a second time with a frightening noise. "Stop it!" This time I shout, but I realize that it is impossible to attract the attention of the medical team, and I abandon my efforts. I take no further interest in my body, which means nothing anymore to me, and

I leave it behind without any regret. I start to experience wonderful sensations. I feel nothing at all except peace, comfort and wellbeing. I get the impression that all my troubles are over, and I say to myself, "How nice it is, how peaceful, nothing hurts."

Suddenly, I think of my parents, and to my great astonishment I find myself immediately in front of them in the kitchen in our house. I don't know how that happened. Simply by willing it, and as if by magic, I've been instantly transported to them. And yet they live a long way from the hospital, more than 170 kilometres. It takes a good two hours to get there by car, because you go through a lot of little villages. They are sitting at the table, eating in silence. Mum is crying. I'm sure she doesn't realize that her tears are running down her hollow cheeks. She looks exhausted. My father is chewing mechanically, his eyes blank. It is a real scene of desolation. "He is going to die," my mother thinks. A fraction of a second later, the same words cross her lips. "At last, she is facing the facts," thinks my father, "what can I do to comfort her?" "Oh no, Louise, don't say that," he says, wincing slightly. "You know quite well that the bone marrow transplant has worked, even if there are complications. That's normal, it happens all the time." I'm no longer astonished to hear their thoughts and to know what they will say before they have spoken. It already seems to me perfectly normal and very simple. I have never seen them in such despair as at that moment, and so isolated in their respective suffering, incapable of facing the disaster together. Seeing my parents so utterly crushed by my imminent death hurts me. Mum keeps on crying silently. The tears bring her no comfort, nothing in the world can console her, that is obvious. She continues to eat and to cry, swallowing her dinner and her tears at the same time, overcome by a sorrow without end and without any possible consolation. She is going to lose this son she loves so much, and she will never get over it. I turn towards my father who has pushed his plate away and lit a cigarette. My illness, my approaching death has broken up their marriage. Some parents of sick children come out of it strengthened, clinging to each other so as not

116

to go under, breathing courage into each other in turn according to the strength each of them has at the moment. But in the majority of cases, couples split up when their child dies. It is too terrible a trial, love is not great enough. I try with all my strength to enter into contact with my parents. I would like to say to them, "Don't cry, I'm all right. I'm happy, at last I'm free and delivered from this body which has given me so many problems during my life," but I don't have the power to do it, in spite of all the strength of my love. I look at them and I feel pain for them, and with them, but in a way that's curiously detached. It's as if I felt empathy for the sorrow of all parents in the whole world who are crying for their dying children.

At this instant, I realize that I'm completely myself, just as when I was still in my body, I simply have more distance from people, as if I understood everything better than before. In fact, I'm more aware of my own identity and my personality than I have ever been. I record that I'm no longer my parents' son, my sister's brother, Olga's cousin, my grandparents' grandson, I'm totally and completely myself. Never in my life have I been so entirely myself, the concentration of the very essence of my inmost authentic being, as at that precise moment when I prepare to leave the world. For I'm absolutely aware that I'm dying.

At the very moment that I realize that I cannot help my parents, I'm sucked into a dark tunnel. An immense force is pulling me upwards at a dizzy speed which gets faster and faster. It is perhaps the speed of a rocket going towards the moon, or may be even faster than that. I'm not running, I'm not floating, it is rather as though I was flowing, but upwards. I experience the feeling of absolute freedom, liberated from the constraints of a physical body that we have to carry around with us all the time on earth. I'm free, I'm happy, I'm well, and I'm not at all frightened. I travel over great distances in a few hundredths of a second, or perhaps it is outside time. There seem to be various presences around me, but I cannot see anyone. Although the tunnel is black, it isn't frightening, but appears to be made of a protective energy. All this time I can hear strange music, very beautiful, very pure, which seems to come from the depths of time and which penetrates me completely. And then, bit by bit, I can see a long way, a very long way, at an incredible distance, a dazzling white light. I'm drawn towards it as if by a magnet; this sensation is so intense and powerful that at that very moment, I give up my earthly life in order to abandon myself to this new and marvellous thing. Nothing, absolutely nothing nor anyone could prevent me from going towards this light which increases as I go towards it at a dizzy speed. The light becomes more intense, even more attractive, and suddenly, I go into it in an explosion of unbelievable joy.

Once I'm inside this brilliant golden light which, however, doesn't dazzle me, I feel a state of completeness. I'm filled with intense feelings as the rays of this light flood into every part of my being. As I absorb this energy, I experience a feeling of blessedness. I'm caught up in a whirlwind that envelops me and covers me, penetrating my whole being. Bathed in this light, I become a fragment of it, yet at the same time remaining myself. I'm submerged in love, my consciousness completely awake for an incalculable length of time. I realize that at last I have come home, I have found my place of origin and I'm filled with infinite joy. Suddenly, from this light a silhouette appears. It takes the form of a person, and yet it isn't a person. I'm aware that the closer this light gets to me, the love becomes greater and more pure. I immediately love it with my whole being. The light becomes me, and I become the light. I have the impression that I exist in it, am part of it, am nourished by it, and this sensation grows inside me, culminating in a radiant feeling of ecstasy and perfection. The emotions that I feel are millions of times more intense than the feeble sensations that I felt on earth. It is much stronger and truer, authentic and eternal. I no longer have a single thought about my earthly life, my parents, my sister or my friends. I'm in a state where only consciousness exists, but what a sublime state of consciousness!

Suddenly, this being of light speaks to me. It doesn't use words but communicates directly with my consciousness. "Show me what you

*have done with your life," it says. I'm aware that it knows perfectly
well, it knows everything about me, but it wants me to realize what
I have done with my life. At once, the regression starts. I can see a
baby in a pram, and from behind, I can see a woman bending over him
and stroking his cheek. I feel the wellbeing of the baby and I realize
that the baby is me. I'm aware of the love and tenderness that this
woman feels for the child, and I see that it is my mother. At the same
time, I'm the baby and the woman, as if I were in the body and heart
of both of them simultaneously. From then on, I start to go forward
through the first part of my life, hour by hour, day by day, week by
week, month by month, and then year by year, until the moment I see
my body inert and pale on the hospital bed. It is all there, absolutely
everything, nothing is missing from this majestic retrospective of my
life. I relive my sentiments and feel those of other people. I understand
the emotions that I provoked in those who were involved in my actions
since I put myself in their place. The reasons for my behaviour are
revealed to me as are those of the people who are part of the scene
that I'm reliving. The being of light is at my side and helps me to
understand and to learn. My perception of the situation is perfect;
I see from everyone's perspective which allows me to be aware of the
causes and consequences of each of my actions, words, gestures, looks,
thoughts — and the related emotions and sensations — for every minute
of my life. The amount of information released is extraordinary and
utterly amazes me. I'm at the same time myself and other people, and
I realize that the good or the ill that I have done to others, I really did
to myself.*

*The review of my life happens as if I were watching a film through a
viewer. The scenes that I'm watching, I can speed up a passage if I
had understood it, slow it down if I want to look more closely, press
the pause button if I want to study an event more thoroughly. I'm the
one who decides, but it is the being of light who orchestrates it all.
Sometimes, the sequences I watch are very painful, mainly because
I'm ashamed of what I have done to other people. In these moments, the*

being of light loves me quite simply all the time it takes for me to bear the consequences of the film of my life. I'm watching a scene which makes me feel particularly ashamed: some years ago, I had broken a Chinese vase that Mum really liked. This vase had belonged to her maternal grandfather, and when he died, Mum had wanted to keep it. All the family had agreed that she should keep this souvenir, for they all knew how much she adored her grandfather. This vase was placed in a corner of the sitting room, high up, in a safe place. But that day I was fooling around with one of my mates, and because I was rushing around like an idiot, I bumped into the piece of furniture on which the vase was standing. It fell and broke into a thousand pieces. I was very much afraid that Mum would be angry, and as my little sister had the bad habit of playing ball in the sitting room, I told Mum that she had broken it. It was really very mean and cowardly on my part, and I have never forgiven myself, but neither did I ever have the courage to own up to the lie. Now I'm reliving the episode, but I also find myself in my little sister's place, and I can feel the incomprehension and great outrage that this injustice caused her, and also her deep sorrow at having been betrayed by me, the brother she loved so much. In the presence of the being of light, I understand it all, her point of view and mine, my nastiness and her despair, and the reasons which made me behave like this.

At this very moment I feel the presence of the being of light intensify. He hasn't left me for a moment since the beginning of the review of my life, but at this precise instant I can feel his protection and his love envelop me more strongly, more closely. It is an energy born of total compassion. He knows all about me and loves me without reserve, unconditionally and absolutely, in spite of all my imperfections, in spite of my cowardice. I have never felt myself to be so protected, completely safe, knowing that no harm will ever happen to me again.

Together we go through all my earthly life. A balance sheet of one's life is a solemn moment. I'm facing remorse and bitter regrets which could crush me and destroy me without the loving help of this being of light, but I also feel the joy caused by the good and generous actions that I have done and of which I'm proud. I realize that to make an evaluation of one's life is difficult when all is finished, and when it is too late to rectify an injustice, or to add on another good action, or say a kind word. I discover that we are responsible for every second of our lives, and this has implications that I shall never forget. We are free to act, we can even commit abominable misdeeds, but one day we shall be confronted by them, inescapably. Like the effect of a boomerang, all that we do will come back to us, unavoidably. During all this time that I'm reviewing my life, the being of light is teaching me what is important, and what is not. The things that I was proud of, successes at school, doing well at sport, victories over other people, don't arouse any approval from him, only indifference. On the other hand, all the events which involve positive interaction with people are regarded as important. The only things that count are the caring ways in which we behave towards others, our compassion and our love of our fellow human beings. No judgement is made by this magnificent being, I'm the one who judges, and this is much more difficult. At the appropriate moment when I am weighed down with the shame of certain aspects of my behaviour, the being of light says to me gently, "You were learning..."

At this moment, I see a man sitting in an armchair in a lounge in the firelight. Two boys are playing on the floor, one with a little car, the other with some wooden bricks which he is trying to put one on top of the other. The man is reading a newspaper, while glancing at the children from time to time. The atmosphere is peaceful, and I'm aware of the love that the father feels as he looks at his children. "Who is this man?" I ask the being of light. "It is you," he replies, "you, much later in your life."

"But I don't want to go back into my body!" I exclaim, and I feel a great sadness, a rebellion tinged with powerlessness. "It is absolutely out of the question for me to return to life. I want to stay here!" I state vehemently. I think of my young life and all the physical problems

121

that I have put up with, and I add, "I'm so pleased that all that is over now."

"You cannot stay," he replies patiently, "you haven't made much of your life yet."

I think over the words that the being of light has put into my mind, and I realize that I understand perfectly what he means. I'm part of a whole, a plan, a project, a masterpiece, I have my part in it, and I will never again feel alone.

This magnificent light appears to refract through a brilliant crystal. You would say that it radiates from the very centre of consciousness in which I find myself, and it shines in every direction through the universe expanding infinitely. I realize that it forms an integral part of all living beings, and at the same time, all living beings also form an integral part of it. I understand that we are all integrated in a single great living universe. My contact with this magnificent presence, whose radiance lights up everything around me, gives me the capacity to access a vast understanding of things, a comprehension which is infinitely superior to anything that I could achieve before. The knowledge and the truth which emanate from the being of light penetrate me, and I become aware that my life has a purpose, and that it forms part of a whole which includes me, and goes beyond me at the same time. Of course, I tell myself, life dwells in consciousness, that is obvious. And this consciousness, which is linked to our personality, continues to live outside the body. Everything becomes clear, all that has happened since the beginning of the world, and all that will happen in the future, and the reason for it all. In the same way, my life has a trajectory which is preordained in its broad outlines and in its extremities, but at any moment several paths are open to me, and I'm free to take one rather than the other. All the possibilities are there potentially, and it is me and only me who decides which I choose. I'm free, but I'm not alone. I'm master of my individual destiny, but caught up in the fate of humanity. By going forward, feeling my way, learning, I gradually discover my course. My path is revealed to me, and I fashion it bit by bit according to my ambitions, my capacities, my desires. All this appears clearly to me as an evidence. Thoughts force themselves upon me in their fullness. They are clear without my needing to make the slightest effort of comprehension. In the presence of this loving, sympathetic being, all is revealed to me. I think of a question, and at once the answer is there in full. It is just as simple as that.

A feeling of my entire consciousness expanding takes hold of me. The boundaries of my thought are shattered, and I'm at last in possession of all my faculties. I enjoy an intellectual power which dazzles and delights me. I understand the meaning of life and death, and the urgent necessity of all events. "But of course," I say to myself, "I knew all that. How could I have forgotten it? It's obvious," and a great feeling of peace comes over me. I decide to find out about the sins I have heard so much about at Sunday school, and which always frightened me. The being of light immediately replies, "Sin doesn't exist. Not in the way you imagine it down there. The only thing that counts here is the way you think. What is there in your heart?" he asks me. In a way that I cannot explain, I'm able to look into my heart and to see that there is only love there. I realize exactly what he means. And I say to him, "Of course," and I feel that it is something that I have always known, but had forgotten until he reminded me. "Of course," I repeat. Then I ask, "Since I cannot stay, since I must go back, I have another question to ask: how does the world work? Why are there children who die, and wars, and all that?" He explains to me again that all the things that happen in the life of each human being, whether they are sad or happy, form part of a coherent plan, which is harmonious and infinitely just. "During life on earth you only see a small part of the picture, you don't get the overall view, so it all seems chaotic and absurd. It is a problem of perspective."

"Of course," I repeat, "It is obvious—during our lifetime we cannot understand."

Suddenly, I'm surrounded by a crowd of people. I don't know them, but they seem to have come for me. I particularly see their faces, they all look happy, it is a joyful occasion, and I know that they have come to protect and guide me. It is as if I were coming home, and they had come to greet me on the doorstep and to welcome me. It all appears beautiful and light-hearted; it is a moment of pure splendour. I talk with some among them using no words, simply from consciousness to consciousness. I ask them what is happening, and I immediately receive a reply mentally. They tell me that I'm not dying, and that I cannot stay, that I must return to my body. Again, I feel an immense rebellion at the idea of having to leave this enchanting place, but they make me understand that it is good like this, and I immediately become calm. I receive an answer at once to all the questions I'm asking, so I have no time to worry about anything. Suddenly, I see my grandmother. She comes forward with open arms as if to embrace me. She is younger and more beautiful than the day she died. I recognize her immediately, although she doesn't really have a body. Her body is translucent with all her limbs, arms and legs, but I don't see her physically, it is rather a recognition by spirit. That seems quite natural to me, and doesn't surprise me at all. We communicate mentally and I feel her great pleasure in seeing me. I know her thoughts instantly, as she knows mine. All this happens as if each one of us had access to the consciousness of the other. There is no room for doubts or misunderstandings, everything is clear.

We start to walk in a huge field, bathed in a light of an unknown intensity, dazzling yet as soft as silk. Flowers are spread like a carpet as far as the horizon. I have never seen such splendid flowers, of colours I have never known, in perfect harmony. It is all infinitely more beautiful, more dazzling, more powerful, than on earth. A little path winds its way to the right, and disappears among the flowers, as it leads towards the horizon. I'm walking along with my grandmother beside me, when I see a small stream. At the other side of it, there are some wonderful horses, about twenty of them. They are galloping, kicking out their legs, a feeling of great power emanates from them, and watching them is a splendid experience. I'm getting ready to jump across the stream when my Uncle Nicolas appears at my side. He isn't really my uncle, he is a friend of the family, but my sister and I have always called him uncle. And yet he is alive, and I don't understand what he is doing here. At the moment that I left my body in my hospital room, I saw the duty team in action around my body, and afterwards, I saw my parents in our kitchen. But since I came into the light after coming through the tunnel, I have only met people who were dead. So, I cannot understand his presence here. He says to me, "Where are you going?" I answer, "I'm going to see the horses, they are so beautiful."

"No, you cannot cross the stream, otherwise you will not be able to return to your body" he explains. "I know that," I reply, "but I don't want to return to my body! I want to stay here. I want to go and see the horses!"

"That isn't possible yet," replies Uncle Nicolas firmly, "Your time hasn't yet come, you can't stay. You aren't dying, because you haven't yet lived the life you were destined to live." I remember the review of my life, and the fact that I shall be a father one day much later on. I know that the limits of my life are fixed, and that I can change nothing. I'm again seized by a deep sadness and I realize that I shall experience nostalgia until the moment when I can at last come back to this marvellous place.

I continue to walk with my grandmother when my cousin Alice appears in front of us. "Alice!" I cry and we fall into each other's arms, with our bodies which aren't really bodies, but above all with our whole being. She is radiant and very joyful. The last time I saw her, the day she died, she was only five months old. I'm not at all surprised to recognize her immediately, although, obviously, she doesn't look at all like the baby she was ten years ago. I know now that where I am, there are no more questions, there are only answers, because understanding is everywhere and in everything. We carry on walking together, all three of us, among the flowers, in perfect harmony. I would like to walk like that to the end of time.

125

Suddenly, a formidable explosion of light occurs in front of me. In the distance, a very long way from where we are, I can see a town. Even at this distance, I realize that it is enormous. Just by wishing to see it more closely, I'm immediately transported there. First of all, I see a street, a very bright street. The only thing I can compare it to is gold, but here it is light, transparent. When you imagine gold, you think of something shining and hard, whereas here everything is gentle and soft. The luminosity in this town comes from the walls, the streets, and the beings who are here, but I cannot distinguish one from the other. Everything in this city is made of light. You could say that the town rests on nothing and has no need of any support. I have the impression that the heart of it resembles a laser beam which is directed at me. A bit further on, I can see a bridge and further still, part of the town formed by an assembly of gilded towers which look like castles. On my left I see a cathedral made wholly of a crystalline substance, lit from the inside by an intense source of light. The building contains a power which seems to throb through the air. The cathedral is entirely made up of information. I'm aware that I'm in a place of knowledge and that I'm here to learn. I can feel it because I'm literally bombarded with information which comes from every direction. It is as if I put my head in a river and each drop of water was part of the universal knowledge which was permeating me. It is obvious that it isn't just a city, but a whole world apart. A perfect order and harmony reign in this place, and I notice an atmosphere of serenity, knowledge and love.

At this moment my eye is caught by a large tall square building made of transparent glass shining with an intense light. I decide to go near to see it, and immediately I find myself in front of the building. As I approach, I see that it contains thousands of books. I'm overcome by an intense desire to know the contents of all these works, and I move nearer. Instantly, the knowledge contained in all these books flows towards me like a wave breaking. I know the answers to all my questions are stored there, and also to all the questions I have never asked: the meaning of life, the human condition, the mystery of death, the reasons for all the injustice and all the ignominy, why so much love is wasted, and the justification for people's despair. But that isn't all, these books also contain all the knowledge that human beings have produced through their own sheer willpower, the discoveries made by researchers in a moment of creative illumination, fruit of their intelligence and of their resolve to improve the lot of human beings. These works also explain how life was born out of a chaotic universe, how it survived against all probability, against all logic, issued from a power superior to natural laws, so that one day mankind could rise up in an environment which has become hospitable and wonderful. The place of humans in the immense universe is explained and their destiny beyond the limits of the physical world. I am seized by an overwhelming urge to understand, stronger than desire, stronger than pleasure, stronger than all human emotions put together. I go towards the door of the library, overcome by a burning impatience to acquire all this knowledge, when a thick fog rises up between me and the entrance to the building. Disorientated, I grope around in the mist eager to find the entrance, when my Uncle Alan, who died two years ago, appears. "James, this isn't the time, you cannot go into the library now," he tells me. "No!" I cry, seized by an immense feeling of indignation which shakes me to the depths of my being, "Don't stop me, I want to understand, I want to go in, I can't live any longer without knowing!"

"Later," he replies, "be patient, the answers to all your questions will be there for you at the right time. Now it is too soon, you have your life to live."

"What is life compared with all the splendour that I've seen here, what's the good of a life of doubt, of ignorance, with insignificant joys, brief pleasures, and all the restrictions of the body?"

"It is for you to create a worthwhile existence, to rise above mediocrity, to make a meaningful life, it's all up to you. The love that you create in your life will have its continuation here. Nothing is lost, nothing is useless, nothing is insignificant."

"Why do I have to wait all those years?" I ask in distress. "Wait?" interrupts Uncle Alan, "no, certainly not! You must fill the years with

purpose, creativity, beauty, love, yes, above all, love. Don't forget that you'll have children later on in your life."

*"It's true," I agree, "I had forgotten again, I'll be a father one day."
I remember the brief moment of happiness and peace that I felt when I saw myself projected into the future sitting in my home with my sons playing on the floor and that comforts me. "All right, I will try, since I have to," I say reluctantly.*

I think over all that I have learnt here and shall never forget. I know now that I can leave my body while still remaining myself, the quintessence of my innermost being, more real and more conscious than in my everyday life. This reality, which I wasn't at all expecting, has made me realize that my life isn't limited to the existence within my body, but that I possess, like all human beings, a future beyond the known limits. I have understood that I'm in my body for the period of my lifetime, but that I'm more than my body. This has many consequences. The injustices are less harsh; they must be borne nevertheless, but they will form part of a wider picture, as part of a global vision, in an understanding that gives comfort.

This perspective gives a meaning to all my actions, past and to come, to all my future efforts, joys and sorrows. If the meaning of my existence isn't only to be measured in the space of my lifetime, then everything falls into place. If what we call life is in reality only the prelude to real life, if what we undertake during our physical existence conditions what we will be in the other life, if there is discontinuity but no end, if there is a transition but not annihilation, if all our actions have a lasting meaning which will not cease with the death of our body, but will continue beyond, if what we make and create in this life will find its place elsewhere, then I will never again feel like a pathetic puppet moving around in an absurd cruel world, a world where children fall ill and die... How lucky I have been to meet a majestic being whom I loved immediately and totally, with all my strength, with all my being, and memory of which will be with me all my life until the infinitely joyful day when I shall meet him again, the day when I shall come home for ever to the place I came from. What harm can ever come to me in my life, armed as I am with all this knowledge, this comfort, this confidence which this magic journey has given me? At the time of the review of my life, the true values were revealed to me, love of one's fellow human being, harmony, tolerance, compassion, humility, creativity, the pleasure of learning and understanding, the joy of savouring the present moment, the veneration of nature. I have also learned that the domination of others is never beneficial and that social status and money are only positive in so far as they serve altruistic and generous causes. I think again of the unconditional love of the being of light, and of the fact that he loves me, despite all my shortcomings. If he, a being of such perfection, can love me as I am, then I too can accept myself. This acceptance of myself will act as a key to open the door which will lead me to other people.

Love, love... What exactly does it mean? This word so over-used means nothing any more—it must find a new meaning and content. It isn't the kind of sentiment which can be genuine and deeply felt, but which nevertheless is frequently cramped and selfish, which binds us to particular people. Very often people love in a conditional self-interested sort of way. No, it is something different... a powerful and generous emotion, a holistic altruistic dynamic which goes beyond individual interest. I have understood that, whilst remaining myself, with my personality and individuality, I'm nevertheless closely connected to all human beings. We interact continually, without realizing it, and it is only in an extension of our consciousness that we realize that we are all one. The encounter with the being of light, which was the quintessence of my journey in the other world, is an illustration of this love. That emotion, for which it would be necessary to coin a new word, creates meaning itself, and seems to be the force that binds together all living beings, the ultimate energy which interconnects all the parts that make up the universe. Love seems also to be closely linked with knowledge, which, while creating order and harmony, increases the intensity of it. I think about my fleeting inroad into this other existence which gave me a wider vision, more real and more accurate, of the world to which I'm getting ready to return to live my life as a responsible, well-informed man. I will have to face the same trials as everyone else, of course, why should I be spared?: the illness that I shall go back to, the selfishness, the wickedness of people, which is only the reflection of their own suffering, betrayals and mediocrity. My own daily struggle will be to face up to the wounds of the world through the enlightenment revealed in this experience of mine. I will spend my life trying to be equal to the teaching that I received and I will find resources in the memory of my magic journey. The fear of death, this burden which human beings carry in their hearts unconsciously but continually, has been lifted from me forever. I remember all the discussions that we had in the hospital, we young patients, which centred essentially on our fear of death, even if that word wasn't often spoken, because we were so much afraid of it. Since I must return to my body, I will be able to tell them what I have experienced and why we mustn't fear death. I shall explain it to them, they will be so happy...

At that very moment, I feel myself sucked backwards by a force from somewhere I cannot tell, and I find myself again in the tunnel which I pass along at an incredible speed in the other direction.

Suddenly, brutally, I go back into my body. Immediately the pain comes back. Agnes is bending over me, looking anxious, peering at my face. When I open my eyes, the look on her face changes, she smiles with relief. She is pleased, but I'm not. I feel this physical reintegration as something psychologically very painful, restricting and frustrating. I immediately become a slave to my body again as I'm reunited with its pain and fragility. I feel myself imprisoned, stifled in this envelope of flesh which deprives me of my freedom. Without it, I was master of my movements. In a state of weightlessness and outside time, I enjoyed the extraordinary privilege of going instantly to any part of the universe simply by wishing it. Now my consciousness, essence of my true and real being, is again enclosed within the narrow confines *of a physical body which weighs me down, restricts me, and takes from me this sublime freedom which I have tasted, and which I shall never forget. All the inherent properties of my existence outside my body are irreparably lost, the unlimited intellectual power which procured for me the infinite joy of understanding everything, and the capacity to transcend myself and to merge with absolute love symbolized by the being of light. My body deprives me of this transcendence of mind which immersed me in endless ecstasy, and the suffering of having lost all that will be constantly with me, I know that. I feel an immense nostalgia for what I have experienced, and I know that it will never leave me. "Are you all right?" asks Agnes, still worried, but already confident again. "Yes and no," I reply, sad and resigned at the same time, aware that my answer doesn't mean anything. "Yes and no, that depends..."*

It is close to midnight when I put down the sheets of paper covered with James's sloping handwriting. I'm dazzled and totally overwhelmed by his account. I put out the bedside lamp and think over for a long time what I have just read. Finally, I lose my grip on reality and feel myself sliding gently into sleep. The next day I rush into James's room at the first opportunity. Thank heavens, he is alone.

23

James is having breakfast in bed and he greets me with a big smile.

"Have you read my letter?" he asks immediately.

And I answer, all excited:

"Yes, I have, and I've got hundreds of questions. First of all, you were wrong, dying isn't 'end of story', as you said?"

James laughs, obliged to admit that I had been right:

"Not only is it *not* 'end of story', it's wonderful. It is the most beautiful thing that has ever happened in my life."

"So, Fiona didn't lie to us? Dying doesn't hurt?"

"No, she was right. At the very moment when I left my body, the intense pain that I'd been suffering for hours disappeared straightaway."

"And you were really not frightened?"

"I wasn't frightened, no, I never felt better in all my life."

"It's wonderful what happened to you. Everybody must know about it, you must tell our friends, our parents, the nurses, they'll all be so pleased."

"You're wrong there! I tried to talk about it to Dr Tomala, my parents, my sister—although she is a little young for that—my cousin Olga, some of the nurses, and one or two of our friends. I was so fascinated by what had happened that I felt I simply had to share it with them. It was so disappointing. Nobody believed me except Agnes. They were condescending, you know, the sort of thing— 'poor lad, he nearly died, he's disturbed, let's pretend to believe him...' I felt misunderstood, a little ridiculed. I told them about the most fabulous moment of my life, and they brushed it away without making the slightest effort to understand me. But it's true that I didn't find the right words to describe what I saw, the words aren't adequate, the message didn't get through."

"Even your parents didn't believe you?"

"No, not even them. All the same they were a bit shaken when I told them I'd met Uncle Nicolas and that I didn't understand what he was doing there since he wasn't dead. Then they were forced to tell me that he'd actually died in a motorbike accident last week. Because I was really ill at the time, they didn't tell me so as not to upset me even more. But they reckoned that it was a coincidence and that it doesn't prove anything."

"A coincidence, really... did Agnes believe you?"

"Yes, because I told her in detail about how they resuscitated me. I listed all the people who came into the room, the order in which they arrived, I described their slightest gesture, and I repeated the words they spoke. At the beginning she was sceptical. She told me it was impossible for me to remember, because I was unconscious and in cardiac arrest. 'You must have been watching that American series *ER* on the TV,' she said to me. 'That's why you can describe a resuscitation. The rest, you just guessed.'

"'Oh, yes?' I replied, 'and how could I have guessed that the doctor was in such a hurry that he mistook your name and called you Blanche?' That threw her, and she was forced to admit it was impossible for me to have got all that information through my normal senses, and so something unusual must have happened. Since then, she believes me, but she's the only one. From now one I shan't speak of my experience unless I'm absolutely sure and certain that the person before me understands. So, I warn you, if you laugh, I'll never talk to you about it again."

"You can talk to me freely and trust me, James, I shan't laugh. *Wet or dry, I'll go to hell if I tell a lie!*"

"Don't use that stupid rhyme, hell doesn't exist. In that at least, I wasn't mistaken. I know now where we go when we die, I've been there. How can I put it...? If you take the thousand best things that have happened to you in your life and multiply them by a million, perhaps you'll get somewhere near that feeling, but even that isn't sure."

"That's funny, I envy you for having nearly died, and yet that's what we're all most afraid of here. You see, I wasn't wrong to dream of a better world waiting for us. How do you imagine life there?"

"I don't know. I've only made a brief incursion into that other dimension. I've experienced the beginning of something, I was drawn into a process which stopped abruptly when I was forced to return to my body. If I'd gone on, I think that what was happening to me would have continued and finally brought me to a state of being that I can't imagine."

"In fact, you were neither alive nor dead?"

"I was clinically dead in the sense that you all understand it. I think I found myself in a sort of antechamber, in a space between life and actual physical death, liberated from the laws of the first, and initiated into those of the second. If you like, I'll give you a simpler example, it's like moving from one room to another in the same house. I can't tell you what this other room will be like. All I know is that I shall go back home one day when I die, and that I shall be infinitely happy. That's all I can say."

"That's a great deal already. That gives us hope and answers a lot of questions that we were asking."

"It answers all mine."

"How do you feel now? Do you feel better?"

"Much better. Anyway, nobody here understands what they're starting to call my 'miraculous recovery'. All the complications I was having with the rejection of the transplant cleared up almost at once, as if by magic, since I woke up. The results of the tests are good and the doctors are flabbergasted. In short, I'm cured."

Suddenly, I envy him enormously. If only I, too, could be cured miraculously...

"How is it possible?"

"It's the being of light who healed me, that's obvious. But I'm not telling anybody that, they already think I'm delusional and crazy. You're different, I can feel that you understand."

134

"Yes, the only thing I didn't understand were the two boys who were playing on the floor. Who were they?"

"They're my sons!"

"You're joking, since when did you have any children?"

"I haven't got any yet, as you well know, but I shall have them."

"Anybody can say that they'll have children one day, me too, perhaps..."

"I didn't *imagine* them, I *saw* them. I was projected into the future, and I experienced a moment in time sitting in an armchair and looking at my two sons. It was quite natural and peaceful. I was a father watching his children playing on the floor and I know that one day in the distant future, I shall live through that very scene, exactly as it was, for the second time, but then it will be in its right place in time. I shall recognize the moment, and I'll remember having lived through it in a flash out of time the day I nearly died. You see, I can't normally imagine what a father must feel. No, that's wrong, I can *imagine* it, but I can't *experience* it, because I haven't got any children at present, and so I don't know the feelings that a father might have when he watches his children playing. You can see that it wasn't something *imagined* but something *experienced,* the difference is obvious."

"That means you won't die of leukaemia? You aren't only in remission, but really cured?"

"Exactly, and when I realized that, I was overcome with a feeling of great sadness."

"Don't you mean great joy?"

"No, a deep and lasting sadness that's inside me all the time. I shall never forget that wonderful place. I often shut my eyes to go back there in my memory, and I'm so happy when I manage to feel a faint reflection of that absolute completeness and love. I'd give everything to go back there, if only for a fraction of a second."

"Perhaps you could do something to go back for a moment?"

"I'm sure I couldn't. I wouldn't know how to go about it, but even if I knew, I wouldn't do it. I didn't have this experience by chance, it happened at an opportune moment in my life, like a gift, like a blessing, like a solution. You don't ask for a present, and you don't demand a blessing, you accept them gratefully and happily when they come."

"Well then, you could commit suicide."

"I would never do that because I have learnt that every life has a purpose, and that we're on earth for a special reason, even if in most cases we don't know what it is. Perhaps it is even impossible to stop a life before the appointed time."

"I have the opposite problem. I don't want to die."

"And yet it wouldn't really be such a great tragedy..."

"Don't say things like that! I didn't know you had so little consideration for me!"

"But it's precisely because I'm so fond of you that I said it."

"Well, that's something new. Before, we were not really close friends, just patients being treated in the same hospital. What's happened to you?"

"That's a good question. I don't understand it myself; I only know that for me today everything is different and I shall never be the same again."

"Will you be better or worse?"

James bursts out laughing, his eyes shining full of kindness, yet at the same time with a strange, faraway look:

"Better or worse, I don't know. What's for sure is that nothing frightens me, neither life nor death, for I know that I shall never die. I shall simply go back home, to my real home."

"Maybe you'll change and become like you were before? You're probably a bit upset at the moment because of all the medication you've been given, and as a result of the shock of dying. Perhaps when you've recovered, you'll be afraid of death again—like the rest of us?"

James answers with a smile:

"No, I shall never again be as I was before. The medication that was injected into my body has nothing to do with it. Don't forget that I had left that body. Dying wasn't a shock but a revelation. It's returning to my body that upset me!"

We remain sitting in silence for a long time. I remember the magic words that Angel repeated so often: "You are in your body, but you are more than your body..." I'm glad that fits so perfectly with what James has experienced. If the same information comes from two different sources, you can allow yourself to begin to believe it. I look at James who has closed his eyes. There are tears on his eyelashes. I know that he's thinking about that wonderful place and that he's sad not to be there anymore, and happy to be returning there one day, even a long time off in the future. It is easier to live in hope.

~

James went home this morning. Yesterday he spent the whole afternoon in my room. We didn't talk much because I was dozing, worn out by this tiredness which really deserves a different name. The word "tiredness" has always meant to me either the end of a happy day in the sunshine spent at the seaside, and the healthy weariness it brings, or waking up painfully on mornings after too few hours' sleep when part of us is still in the land of dreams. But the tiredness I feel today is exhaustion, depression and devastation. It leaves me gasping for breath, staggering, incapable of gathering my thoughts and expressing myself. So, James stayed near me in silence; he understood. He smiled at me with this new light in his eyes which wasn't there before his visit to the other world. He has become more than a friend, a real brother who will be with me on the most important and most difficult journey of my life. "I'll call you every day," he promised me. "And if I get worse, will you come and see me?" I asked. "I'll come," he replied without hesitation. "And if I die?"

"I'll come, don't worry, I'll be there," he said without being frightened by the question. How lucky he is to have been cured so miraculously, I said to myself as I slid into the hazy state that comes over me more and more often.

24

A few days later James came back to see me and we at once carried on with our conversation. With him it's no longer a question of talking about trivial things, he only discusses essential matters, as if he had no time to waste. And yet he has more than I do.

"Some curious things have happened to me since I died," James says, "*died* in the sense that everybody understands it, of course."

"Don't keep saying that you died, you nearly died, I know, but you weren't dead, otherwise you wouldn't be here."

"I don't agree. As I told you the other day, I was clinically dead because I was in cardiac arrest for several minutes; Dr Tomala confirmed that. But it doesn't matter, the line between life and death is narrow in any case. Just listen to what I have to tell you. On Sunday night I dreamt that our caretaker was going to die the next day. And yet he wasn't old or ill, so I didn't know if I should believe my dream. The next day when I went home, I saw an ambulance in front of the block of flats and a group of people. I couldn't see who was on the stretcher, but the neighbours told me that the caretaker had fallen ill. He died soon afterwards in hospital of a heart attack. So, I know now that I should trust my dreams."

"That's quite astonishing. Did you like him?"

"No, not especially. He was grumpy and shouted at my friends and me when we made too much noise playing on the grass outside the flats."

"Did you feel sad for him?"

"No, not at all, there's nothing sad about death."

"You just say that because you didn't like him."

"No, that's nothing to do with it. I should say the same thing if my mother had just died, I would simply be upset not to have her with me anymore."

"This dream, was it perhaps just a coincidence?"

"You sound just like my parents, a coincidence—really!"

"What's the point of dreaming about people's death in advance?"

"I don't know. If I were to have another premonition of an imminent death in a dream, I should probably be uneasy if I came across the person I'd dreamt about, who didn't yet know what was going to happen to them during the day... I suppose these dreams have a purpose if they serve to prevent some unfortunate accident, a fire, or whatever. I can tell you about other weird things that have happened to me since I came out of hospital."

"Other premonitions of death?"

James laughs:

"No, more subtle experiences, more difficult to describe. When I walk by buildings, for example, in my road, I can feel what's happening there, the arguments that are going on, the insults that people are shouting at one another, the boredom felt by the elderly, the loneliness of people. I say that I can feel all that, not that I can hear it. The awareness of it is direct, immediate... and quite painful. So, to sort myself out, I go and walk by the river, a long way from the town and the unhappiness of people."

"That can't be easy for you."

"No, it's difficult and I still don't see the sense of it. I've become very sensitive. Really simple things disturb me, a violent film on the television, an argument between my sister and her friends, ordinary things. It is as if I took words at their literal meaning, whereas before I didn't attach much importance to them, like anyone else. In short, nastiness, violence and aggressiveness affect me deeply now."

"You'll have to get used to it again."

"No, I don't think so. In any case I don't want to."

"Have you really changed that much?"

"Yes, I feel much closer to people, and I have feelings of sympathy, and even empathy for them. For example, I happen to know exactly what state of mind a person is in, without talking to them, without even knowing them, just by looking at a passer-by in the street..."

"You really mean that you can *guess* their thoughts, don't you?"

"No, their emotions impose themselves upon me. I'm aware of their thoughts, from the inside, as if I myself were that person, as if I were living their life."

"And that never happened to you before your heart stopped?"

"Never, no. I never used to pay much attention to people, I didn't even see them."

"So now you feel closer to people?"

"Yes and no, both at once. In one way, I feel close to people that I meet or come across, as I just told you. In another way, I'm completely apart from everyone. I'm having a lot of difficulty getting used to my family and friends again, because I don't have the same worries and desires as them anymore. I often feel very much alone."

"What desires do you have?"

"Mainly to return to that wonderful place, full of gentleness... I want it so much, you can't imagine! I'm often overcome by a wave of nostalgia that sweeps over me, delights me and destroys me at the same time. What's more, I frequently get the impression I'm not in my body. Don't take me for a fool, just try to understand. My spirit is elsewhere, as if it lived beside my body, and I have to make a great effort to try to pull it all back together."

"That's a lot of strange things..."

"I know, that's why nobody understands me. You know this experience has completely bowled me over. It's a gift that I've received, but now I have to integrate it into my life, or rather I have to reintegrate my life in spite of the gift. It's very complicated."

"How do you see your future?"

"I don't know yet, for the moment I'm thinking about it. First of all, I want to learn lots of things. At the time of my journey into the other world, everything was obvious, very clear, the answers to all the questions came easily. However, when I woke up, I had lost not the memory, but the substance of all this knowledge. And I want to find it again, at least partially. I have a great thirst to understand and to learn. It is so good to know."

"What will you study? What job do you want to do?"

"It's too soon to tell. At the moment I just feel a bit lost, as if I were no longer the old James, but not yet the new one. I think I'll choose a job that will let me take care of other people. What's vital for me is to live in harmony with what I learnt during my journey into the other dimension. That experience is useless if it doesn't help me to put into practice the values which it taught me. I want my life to be useful, but I don't know yet how I shall manage it, apart from being the father of two boys..."

"So, you're still at the same point as before, you still don't know what you want to do with your life?"

"I know what I *don't* want to do with it! Before, my dream was to earn as much money as possible. My parents haven't got much money, and I envied some of my friends who had everything they wanted, the latest electronic devices, travel... nice things, but when all is said and done, trivial. Today, I know that money isn't interesting unless it lets you realize useful projects and above all, unless it's shared."

"Wait until you see a friend with a brand-new snowboard, or a motor scooter, you might change your mind..."

"No, you still don't understand. I'm not the same any more, even if I don't know yet who I am..."

25

The next day James arrives after lunch, and settles down in the armchair beside my bed. He had promised to keep me company no matter how my illness developed, and he's keeping his word. I still want him to talk to me about his new vision of life that pleases me so much.

"Explain to me some more about what's changed in your life," I say to him.

"Everything, absolutely everything, I don't even know where to begin... First of all, I'm no longer afraid of death, obviously. Do you remember the discussions we had in the common room? We all really got the wind up thinking how our illness would develop and the possibility of a fatal outcome. That terrible worry has completely and definitively disappeared from my life."

"It's normal that you're not scared any more, you're no longer ill!"

"I'm cured, it's true, but that has nothing to do with it. Anyway, I could have an accident or get another disease and one day I shall die, like everybody else. I'm not afraid of death anymore, because I know it doesn't exist! I've made a brief incursion into that other world, and I know that one day I'll at last be able to return there forever."

"What else has changed?"

"Now I accept myself as I am, and that gives me lots of confidence. Other people's opinions no longer affect me, their expectations won't change anything in the way I will live my life."

"I'm always influenced by other people. Where does this self-confidence come from?"

"When I reviewed my whole life in the presence of the being of light, I understood that he loved me quite simply as I am, in spite of all my shortcomings. If a being of such splendour can love me as I am, then I can accept myself. My self-confidence comes from that."

"Tell me about this love."

"It's an emotion that surpasses anything you know, anything you can imagine. The love of this being of light overwhelmed me totally like a wave breaking, filling me with bliss, saving me forever from my loneliness. I shall never feel lost again, because I know that he will be in my heart at every moment of my life. As soon as this being of light appeared to me, I loved him immediately and completely, more than I have ever loved anybody."

"Did you love him more than your parents?"

"Infinitely more, that has nothing to do with it."

"I thought you loved your parents."

"I love them, of course, but you must understand that in that other world emotions are amplified to infinity. They are so much more powerful and true than the feeble sensations that we have here. That love is beyond words. I'll spend my whole life trying to become better, not to please other people, but in memory of the love of this wonderful being."

"Since everything has been forgiven, why must you make such an effort to improve?"

"The being of light forgave me, that's true, but that doesn't mean that I've forgiven myself. Now I know I'm responsible for every one of my actions, each word, each thought, at every moment. The totality of my life is recorded somewhere and will come back to me one day like a boomerang, the day that I leave this world. I'll no longer have the excuse of not knowing, because I do know."

"It's easier not to know."

"Probably, but that's the price of responsibility."

"On the other hand, since you've learnt so much, it must be easy for you to live as you should."

"To live as I should... That's a bit vague. No, it's just as difficult. I've learnt a lot of things, that's true, but I have to find my way by myself all the same. The experience I had lights the way, but that in itself isn't enough, I've got to transform it into a lifelong project. That's the only thing that frightens me today."

"Which means?"

"That I might not succeed, that I don't find the way, that I can't live up to the splendour that I have seen."

"You've just said that you've got great confidence in yourself."

"That's right, the judgement of other people doesn't affect me anymore, but that doesn't take away the responsibility for giving meaning to my life. What's certain is that I would never again be able to harm other people without realizing the consequences."

"What do you mean?"

"Before this experience of mine, I knew I was making my parents unhappy when I disobeyed them, or that one of my friends got angry if I annoyed him. But there's a huge difference between guessing what another person feels and *experiencing* it in their place. I have learnt that, and now I have to take it into account. I'll probably still be disagreeable to other people at times, or worse, but I'll be aware of the consequences of my actions. I'll no longer be able to say I don't know, because I *do* know. I also think I'll forgive people who hurt me more easily."

"Why?"

"I think I shan't take it so seriously. I shall perhaps tell myself that people are unhappy if they need to be nasty. I shall think about things objectively and perhaps I shall even want to console them."

"That's going a bit far!"

"Not really. People who are happy don't need to hurt others, and those who are unhappy need help."

"I don't believe you. Are you sure you aren't turning into a saint?"

James exclaims with a big laugh:

"Of course not! But I've learnt to put things in perspective and to see them as a whole."

"Could you forgive someone who really made you suffer?"

"I can't swear to it, it's never happened to me, but I'm sure that my capacity to forgive has been multiplied by at least a million."

I start laughing, incredulous:

"As much as that? Tell me, in your view, why did you have this experience?"

"I have no idea, but I know that it wasn't due to chance. I'm just really happy it happened to me."

26

My parents spend the afternoon at my bedside. They try all the time to entertain me by telling stories to amuse me. I know they'd really like to see me laugh, even just for a short while. I too want a bit of frivolity, a breath of fresh air in this heavy day, but it's become difficult for us to joke together. Lightheartedness vanished the moment my illness was diagnosed more than a year ago. We do our best to enjoy ourselves together in spite of the sadness that so often overwhelms us. I like these hours spent in their company. Even if our apparent cheerfulness is rather forced, a bit artificial, it comes, nonetheless, from our fierce determination to snatch a few moments of happiness in these dark days.

They've just left and I'm plunged into a state of torpor, between waking and sleeping. I can hardly feel my body any more, maybe because of the drugs I've been given. In fact, I think it is mainly because I'm no longer interested in it. On the other hand, I'm completely centred on myself, and I'm both astonished and happy to come into contact with the part that is buried deep down inside me. Curiously, when I resonate with my essential true being, I feel detached from my body, and never have I understood Angel as well as now. Yes, I think that I'll be able to escape from this body, now I feel that it's possible.

Evening has fallen and Angel is waiting for me, lying on my pillow, ready to talk. I'm glad, because questions are buzzing around in my head. James's story has left me with a multitude of questions.

"I thought it would be horrible to die and yet there is James talking about it as if it were something marvellous."

"Seeing someone die can be agonizing, that is certain, but what the dying person feels is exactly the opposite of the impression it gives. If you had seen James's lifeless body at the time of his cardiac arrest, his face contorted with pain, you would doubtless have been frightened, and you would have concluded that dying is terrible. And yet, that is the exact opposite of what happened to him. Dying has two aspects, what people see from the outside can indeed be scary and inspire compassion, but what the person who is dying feels is marvellous. But as long as one hasn't experienced it, one cannot know. So, James has done you a real favour by telling you what he felt. You'll never again have the same idea of death."

"I don't understand all these weird things that happen to him. How could he have known the caretaker would die the next day?"

"His journey into the other world liberated abilities he already had, new ways of perceiving with unexpected consequences. All human beings have the potential for these abilities, but they are dormant. All it needs to activate them is to have one's consciousness widened, like what happens when one has a close brush with death."

"I almost thought that he'd become an extraterrestrial with supernatural powers!"

Cheerfully, Angel bursts out laughing:

"Not at all! There's nothing supernatural in it. It is simply a matter of the activation of a natural potential inherent in all humans."

"Why has James changed so much since his cardiac arrest?"

"The truest values have been revealed to him, the importance of love and knowledge, the veneration of life, compassion, unselfishness. While he was reviewing his life, he understood that the fundamental test of human conduct is love. Actions performed with love and genuine feeling are essential. He knows now that every day, every instant, every minute must be lived with as much love, joy and tolerance as possible. James has become aware that he's responsible for his life and his actions, and that one day he must answer for them. Not before a vengeful God, but before his own conscience. Knowing this, he has all he needs to build a meaningful life, but it's up to him to succeed."

"Why does he suddenly want to learn so much? He told me he hated school before his illness."

"I don't think he was talking about that sort of learning. He has come back with the memory of having contemplated the secrets of the universe from the beginning to the end of time, of having discovered the mystery of space and time, of having seen the perfect harmony of all things, and the bonds that unite all beings. During this experience he understood the meaning of all life and of his own in particular. He has the memory of all this, but he forgot the details the moment he came back into his body. Now, quite naturally, he wants to regain as much of that knowledge as possible."

"Wait, wait... You're going too fast for me. What do you mean by 'secrets of the universe'?"

"During James's experience, absolute knowledge was revealed to him: the laws that govern the world and the universe with all their possibilities. In the revelation that gripped him, all the truths found their precise and accurate place in relation to one another, interdependent in permanent movement and transformation. The great religious, spiritual and philosophical movements are all founded on the vision of a peaceful harmonious whole, in a constant interaction, each one bearing part of the truth. Each vision or point of view integrated into the multiple reality, moving within it, is full of meaning through its relationship to all the others, neither more nor less worthwhile than the others. The balance is perfect, but once they are brought down to earthly consciousness, cut off from their context and their interdependence with the others, these visions risk losing their part of truth."

"Do all people go into this other dimension when they die?"

"Remember... the being is absolute; the human condition is only one of its facets. By leaving their physical body behind, they change dimension and take on a new form of expression, characterized by the specific properties inherent in this new state. No one is excluded, of course, since through its nature each being is absolute."

"Who is this being of light?"

"I cannot give you a definite answer. It is perhaps an emanation of God; it is perhaps God... What I'm saying is rather vague, for God is a concept and each person sees it in the way meaningful to them. James wasn't face to face with a concept but with absolute truth, which is very different. What's certain is that there was a radiant intelligence which knew everything about him and loved him infinitely. In the presence of this light James understood that in their essence, all human beings are made of that same substance. He told himself: 'It is us; we are it; it is everywhere, it is boundless...'"

"Has James become this light?"

"Yes, he was fused with it while still keeping his individuality."

"This light, is it even here on earth, do you think?"

"Absolutely. James made a journey into the absolute consciousness and he understood that fragments of this consciousness are to be found in every human being. That's why he feels so certain about the unity of life, this impression he has of being bound to all living beings, this empathy with people. The being of light has taught him that all human beings are one and that this unity is perfect."

"Is that why he can put himself into the head and heart of people, even those he doesn't know?"

"Indeed, even if he does nothing to bring about this phenomenon which in fact only occurs occasionally. While James was reviewing his life, he realized that there existed no real separation between himself and others. 'We are all part of a universal whole in which we are interdependent,' he told himself. 'I am at the same time myself and them, I understand my own point of view and theirs, I feel my emotions and theirs... They are part of me as I am part of them.' While human beings are involved in their everyday pursuits, they don't know it, of course, but in this enhanced state of consciousness inherent in the imminence of death, they realize that their apparent isolation as individuals is an illusion. This is doubtless the reason why James feels empathy with other people's emotions, why he knows their thoughts, their preoccupations, their distress, and their joy as well. Everything happens as if the barrier that separated him from other people and kept him confined in a reduced space had crumbled away during his cardiac arrest. Sometimes he is in a perfect symbiosis with other people, without him choosing neither the time nor the place. He has learnt compassion and that has given him the desire to help other people. His choices in life will depend on it, that is certain. The job he will choose, the way he behaves, the way he lives, will all follow from it."

"Did he understand all that during the experience?"

"No, this knowledge was already hidden in him, as it is in every human being, but he wasn't aware of it. Once he was in that other world, he said to himself: 'But of course, I knew it, how could I have forgotten it...' It became evident to him. At the time of his journey, he rediscovered the place he came from which is the source of all knowledge. By going back there he remembered."

"James talked to me a lot about this strange, powerful love which I don't know..."

"The light has instilled in him a conviction which emerges gradually and is seen more clearly each day. It becomes obvious to him that in the world there is only love and fear, and that human beings are free to choose one or the other. By choosing love, they rid themselves of fear forever."

"I thought that the opposite of love was hatred."

"No, the opposite of love is fear. The fear of not being loved, the fear of being betrayed, the fear of being abandoned. By accepting the unconditional love offered to them, human beings can free themselves from fear and live in harmony with one another."

"But that's not at all what happens in the world."

"I know."

"The people who decide to start wars, the presidents, the generals or I don't know who, do you think they would still make war if they knew what James learnt during his experience?"

"I don't see how they would be able to reconcile these actions with their conscience."

"Just think of it, a better world, a better world here! That's something to dream of, isn't it?"

"Yes, you're right, that is something to dream of, but I repeat that truth is hidden inside every human being, all it takes is a trigger to reveal it."

"James was in cardiac arrest for only a few minutes. How was he able to understand so many things in such a little time?"

"He is grasping all the fullness of his experience bit by bit. Every day he understands the consequences a little better."

"But his journey into the other world seemed quite a lot longer than the few minutes that his cardiac arrest lasted."

"His experience occurred in a dimension where time doesn't exist."

"The existence of this other world, — how can we know if it is true?"

"James knows, he's been there, he has had a direct experience of it. He knows for sure that another world exists where life isn't only real but a lot more beautiful than here. For you it is more difficult, you cannot base it on experience."

"You have to believe it, is that it?"

"That's not what I would say. I don't think it is a question of faith, it is more like an option to choose, or a wager to take..."

"So, I'm totally dependent on James's testimony?"

"No, not at all, you are free. You alone are the judge of what you make of this story. The decision is yours. You know perfectly well that everyone must find the way to their own truth, nobody can do it for them."

27

I stay awake for a long time, looking at the stars which I can see through the window of the hospital room. Today, nothing is the same as before, a universe of beauty and wisdom has been revealed to me through James's story, and Angel's explanations. I realize that during my carefree years, I didn't learn much. I understood ordinary things a bit, I acquired theoretical knowledge at school, but I was never introduced to anything really important. I surprise myself thinking that thanks to, not despite, my illness, I'm finally touching the very essence of life. It is at the very moment when I'm getting ready to leave the world that I'm starting to understand how it works and to see in it the intense beauty and fragility of the human condition. My illness has brought about an accelerated learning, a heightening of consciousness which goes far beyond my age, a revelation which is reserved for those who have little time at their disposal. I'm aware that, not being able to enjoy the usual length of a lifetime, my education has been accelerated, ignoring normal chronology, giving me lessons which I need now, urgently, so that I can face my immediate future. The minutes that I live correspond to hours, the days I spend are like months, even years. Time doesn't pass in the same way for those who are healthy as for sick people at the end of their life. For me there is an urgency, an urgency to learn, to understand, to prepare for tomorrow.

I no longer pay much attention to hospital life, to the treatments that follow one another relentlessly, the care that is lavished upon me with as much concern as at the beginning of my illness. The medical team takes care of my body, but I'm concentrating on the future of my soul, on my evolution as an absolute being destined to take on another of my facets, characterized by a happiness whose fullness I can only guess. If I didn't know what I do know, how lost and desperate I should be...

Nevertheless, everything isn't quite clear yet, it isn't all transparent. Angel is, as ever, indispensable...

"I imagined that heaven, or the other dimension, I don't know what word to choose, was different from anything we know. But according to James's experience, it's very much like our world, even if it's a million times more beautiful."

"At first sight you might think that the other dimension is a sublime replica of life on earth. However, the resemblance shouldn't delude you. To take those images literally would be a mistake. James found himself in a dimension which is incomprehensible to the human mind, so it's represented in such a way that he can understand it."

"So, it happened in his imagination?"

"No, absolutely not! This other world exists, it is real, but it's so different from anything that a human being can conceive that it's transposed into images which are familiar. Your capacity to understand is limited by what you know, so this other reality is adapted to your own."

"What he experienced, is it real or not?"

"It is real. James experienced an event, essential and bewildering, which will determine the rest of his life. He's already been profoundly transformed and will be more so in the course of time."

"Perhaps we can be equally transformed by something which simply happens inside our head?"

"You're right, but this experience didn't come from his imagination. What James experienced has to be seen as evidence. Evidence isn't proof, it is impossible to demonstrate it. Anyway, he isn't trying to convince anyone, he's just trying to share his experience with those who are open to receive it, and who want to listen to him."

"And yet he met deceased members of his family, his grandmother, his cousin, his uncles... Those weren't images."

"It wasn't a question of images, that's true. I think those beings had put on almost earthly appearances without really being so, so that he could recognize them. They are in the other world, but in a form that he wouldn't be able to understand if they hadn't presented themselves in ways that are familiar to him. But perhaps it is only the *telling* of what he perceived which is human, which has to be human since he's here in flesh and blood to talk to you about it."

"Finally, this other world, is it different from or identical to our own? I'm not sure that I have really understood."

"It is by nature fundamentally different, but it was represented in a way that would be comprehensible to James."

"Why make it all so complicated? Why not say this other world is just as he saw it?"

"Because what he saw is only part of the truth, the reality is much more complex."

"James told me something that intrigued me. He said that from now on he'll find it easier to forgive people who do him harm. How is that possible?"

"This awareness probably stems from the review of his life. The being of light helped him to forgive himself everything, his little bad deeds, as well as the big ones. This insight is in him, and he will never forget it. The review of his life has healed all his wounds. The moments of his life when he felt misunderstood or rejected, the actions that hurt him, all these events which caused him to be angry and frustrated, they all lost their importance when he understood the *reason* for them. This review of his life put the missing pieces into the puzzle of his existence. To understand the other person, even if they are wrong, even if they hurt you, is to forgive them, or almost."

"So, he really doesn't want that person to pay for the hurt done to him?"

"No, I don't think so. He will probably tell himself that that person will one day be confronted with their deeds, and will understand at that moment. The thirst for revenge does no good, it only prolongs the suffering. The best response to those who hurt you is to be happy."

"Do you think James has become a sage?"

Angel bursts out laughing:

"Certainly not! Well, at least he won't manage it all the time. Sometimes he'll let his anger get the better of him, and will want to get his own back like everyone else. But it won't last. His encounter with the being of light will act as a compass guiding him all his life."

"Explain to me why he has become so sure of himself."

"That isn't really the right expression. He has learnt to accept himself as he is, but that doesn't mean that he doesn't need to improve himself. In the presence of that being of light, he understood that he was loved, infinitely, unconditionally, just as he is. I'm not talking about love as it is normally understood, this rather changeable feeling which comes and goes mysteriously, which is often conditional, and at times selfish. No, I'm talking about a powerful emotion, an omnipresent universal energy which encompasses everything, which is the source and the end of all things. Of all the lessons that James has learnt, the most important is the primacy of love. The being of light taught him that love is the true nature of human beings. What is it that prevents them from feeling it? What is this barrier that separates them from it? It is essentially their own judgement which they pass on themselves all the time, without pity, without compassion. But remember that the being of light didn't judge James, he loved him. He taught him, not a narcissistic love which could have an arrogant, self-satisfied side to it, but the capacity to accept himself as he is. Once this is established, he is free to go towards the others, without fear, in all confidence. The being of light has cut away the chains of the prison in which he—like most people—had shut himself."

"Is he free now?"

"Yes, without a doubt. Before, he was just like anybody else, carrying a sack heavy with questions on his back, weighing him down, making him sometimes feel sad and anxious. Now he feels relieved, made lighter by his experience which has allowed him to adopt a much more detached attitude."

"How did he deserve to be so privileged?"

"He isn't privileged. Millions of people throughout the world have had the same experience. There is nothing esoteric or extraordinary about it, quite the contrary. It's completely normal, inherent in the human condition. This experience teaches that the being of light loves all human beings in the same way. If only they knew how much they are loved, they would never again feel so frightened and alone."

28

I'm very weak and finding it hard to breathe. The oppression that I experience all the time makes me feel that I'm going to suffocate. Professor Granger requests an X-ray which confirms his fear. I'm suffering from an infection in the respiratory tract. I wasn't mistaken, my condition is worsening. I feel the need more and more urgently to broach the subject of my death with my parents. In any case it already slipped in between us a long time ago, it is present in all we say, in each smile, in each hidden tear. I know they know, but do they know that *I* know? The words I cannot express give me the impression of suffocating just as much as my infection does. When people love one another, they must be able to share everything, even the most difficult things. What's more, a further problem is added to my confusion. I'm afraid of speaking to them, not only because it is sad, not only because it will hurt us, not only because once the fatal issue is expressed clearly, we can no longer pretend to be ignorant of it... No, what really frightens me is that if they consented to let me go, I would die. At the moment, I'm convinced that I cannot die because their love, and their unwillingness to face my impending death, are preventing me. On occasions that comforts me, other times it burdens me. When hope comes tiptoeing back, when exhaustion allows me a little respite, I'm infinitely grateful to them for anchoring me so firmly to this world. However, when I can see no way out of my situation nor the point of continuing to struggle, I feel angry with them for preventing me from setting off for my new destiny.

My rebellion has almost entirely subsided, but certain questions still haunt me at times. I need to discuss them with Angel. Now I can talk to her as soon as I feel the need, she is listening all the time.

"Why was James cured miraculously and not me?"

"Each human being has their path and their destiny. From the human perspective, it is impossible to know the reasons."

"Your answer doesn't really help me."

"You remember our game, the one that envisages the absolute being...."

"Yes, of course I remember. You said that, according to the state you're in, you have more or less power over things."

"Yes, you could put it like that. Each facet—or form of expression—of the absolute being would have certain properties or characteristics belonging to it. According to the state that is active, the characteristics proper to it are also activated. The state of the human being is probably the one with the most limited characteristics. So, mankind only has access to a partial perspective and, therefore, to a limited understanding. At the time of his cardiac arrest and the experience that followed because of it, James had access to an enlarged knowledge which allowed him to understand many things. So, he found himself in a state of his being—and in a dimension—in which he had greater powers."

"How does that help me understand why James got better and not me?"

"Here we face the problem of perspective. Do you remember our analogy about the valley and the summit of the mountain? Depending on the perspective at your disposal, you're able to see—or understand—certain things or not. The being in the human state only has access to a partial perspective and so has only a limited comprehension. According to the characteristics inherent in the state which is activated, the being can apprehend all the aspects or merely some of them, it is contextual. When human beings leave the body, they take on a different facet and thus change dimension, which allows them to have a higher perception of the world and of their human condition. They then understand the reason and the necessity for the pattern of their life."

"What you're telling me is that I shan't be able to understand why I haven't got better while I'm alive?"

"While you are in your present state of life, that of a human being, yes, exactly."

~

I spend a disturbed night with periods of waking followed by long bouts of sleepiness. For some weeks now, the nights haven't brought me any rest. After the midday meal, my parents arrive with a magnificent bouquet of flowers. They know I love flowers more than ever, and that I spend a long time looking at them. We've become much more distant recently, not because we love one another less, but because we can no longer manage to communicate. I take my courage in both hands and decide to tackle the problem. "Dad, Mum, I think the time has come to talk about my death." I wouldn't have wanted to inflict these terrible words on them, and I would certainly have wished to have no reason to say them. "You are just going through a bad patch, my darling," says Dad smiling sadly, "that's normal. This infection of the respiratory tract has really come at a bad time, but Professor Granger is optimistic. He told me so again yesterday and I trust him."

"Professor Granger knows nothing about the time of my death, Dad, I'm the only one who can feel what's happening in my body."

"Don't talk so tragically," whispers Mum, sobbing quietly.

"I'm not talking tragically, Mum, the tragedy has been here for more than a year, since this rotten thing got into my body, for some reason that I cannot understand just yet."

"All you need is to wait till the antibiotics work on this infection," went on Dad, as if he hadn't understood the sense of my words. "Then with the help of the chemotherapy you'll get better."

"Dad, listen, I beg you, listen to me, Dad. I don't think this infection has just come at a bad time; I think rather that it is the end of my illness. I don't think the antibiotics can have any effect, because I feel I'm going to die before they can." I want to talk to them about James's experience, but I can see that it's too soon. Their unconscious refusal to listen to me is so strong that my words wouldn't succeed in piercing the wall put up by their rejection of reality. I feel immensely alone and sad. We all three cry, but each one of us is isolated in their own solitude, infinite and glacial. What has happened to our happy family...?

Luke comes to wish me goodnight, as he does every evening. I'm happy to see him, his smile does me good. Since I've been too weak to go to the common room, the days pass even more slowly, and every distraction is a joy. Luke looks at me closely, and I can see the anxiety in his eyes. He pulls himself together quickly, and smiles again to reassure me. He stays longer than on the other evenings and talks to me about one thing and another, patting my hand from time to time. At last, he wishes me "sweet dreams" and goes away, I'm sad to see him leave.

~

I've just put down the phone, my parents call me every evening to wish me goodnight. At the time when my illness was first diagnosed, they promised to be by my side, and they've kept their word. I think of them with tenderness and gratitude. Although each one of us has often been shut away in their grief, and at times submerged beneath their sorrow, I know that they have supported me as well as they could. They love me dearly, even if they haven't always found the words I needed to hear. Love doesn't come with "directions for use", but it forges the essential bond between people. I think about the months that have gone by, about the trials that I've gone through, the violent and marvellous bursts of hope which have overwhelmed me at times, followed by periods of deep depression. Then little by little, peace has come into my life. Timidly at first, alternating with periods of rebellion, bitterness, despair, and then more often, more and more solidly, to culminate in an unforeseen and magnificent serenity. Now I have certainty that hope doesn't depend on my state of health, but that it is to be found beyond my body. I contemplate the path I have followed and I wonder what will be the next step to take, what I must do to reap the fruits of my efforts. I decide to put this question to Angel, she will know.

"You've often told me that misfortune makes you grow... what's the use of growing if you die all the same?"

"Try to imagine death or the 'passage' as a school exam. The preparation for death is a trial, that's for sure, it demands all your awareness, all your strength, all your clarity of mind."

"I've tried so hard not to panic, not to give way, to be on top of the situation, in order to try to overcome the illness. If all this leads to nothing, what will have been the use of all my struggling?"

"Let's look again at this image of death as a school exam. You have to sit for it, but you can pass the test easily, or not so easily, with more or less success. If you were moving to a new school in a far-off country which required an admission test, do you think what you've learnt here would help you?"

"I think so."

"Not only would it be of use to you in your entrance exam to your new school, but also, it would help you in your studies, your activities and your life. All that you've learnt through your courage, perseverance and lucidity will remain with you. Nothing will be lost; everything will stay with you and be useful to you."

"So, nothing is in vain?"

"No, absolutely nothing! The knowledge that you've acquired is your best friend to face the term ahead of you. Not a bit of your struggle was useless, each second of your path of suffering and apprenticeship will find its justification in a future beyond the limits of human knowledge. You will remain yourself, with your discoveries, your awareness, your progress, the triumphs which have crowned your intense and ceaseless quest to understand."

29

The next morning, I come round with difficulty from a heavy, disturbed sleep. I shall soon die, my body has reached the limit of its resistance, the end of its affliction. And yet I myself am alert, in full possession of my awareness and my intelligence. Yes, now I understand Angel, and I agree with her: I'm inside my body, but I'm more than my body. It has reached the end of its journey, but I haven't. At last, I project myself beyond my physical limit, I discern the existence of another perspective, I can see the path. I know, yes, I'm convinced that I shall not dissolve into nothingness, that I shan't disappear into a cold impersonal cosmic void, that I shan't just merge into an infinity of atoms joining and rejoining in an endless robotic dance. No, I'm something else, I've made my mark upon the world and on those I have loved, and who have loved me. My passage on earth has left indelible traces, I'm a unique being. An infinite feeling of comfort comes over me, nothing has been in vain, not a single bit of suffering or pain, not an instant of loneliness and intense anguish has been useless, everything has meaning, everything is harmonious, integrated, unavoidable and just. I didn't manage to accept this during the long months of my illness when I was still hoping to escape from the inevitable, and even now, at this very moment, I have doubts, feelings of rebellion, questionings, such is the human destiny. But in the depths of my being, I know I can trust, relax and abandon myself to the magic of the impenetrable. There is more than what is known, better than what is revealed. What we can see obscures the evidence, like a veil covering and hiding the truth which lies beyond the visible, like the sun preventing us from seeing the universe in its infinity, spangled with innumerable stars. All the most fundamental things in life are difficult to access. Any certainty which allows us to live and to die with dignity as a full human being comes from what is best in us, born of the quintessence of our truth. Yes, I have learnt all that during my illness, Angel was right when she predicted that hardship makes us grow. I have been so worried since the day I realized that I could die, that horrible morning when I lost so much blood in that splendid hotel on the island of Zakynthos. Since then, the anguish hasn't often left me, because I thought I ought to do something, go somewhere, decide about things I didn't understand. Now I know that dying is quite simple. All I need to do is to let myself go, to loosen my grip, to rest and to let my destiny be fulfilled. It is the opposite of a voluntary step; it is an act of trust.

~

James comes in to see me every day now, he's sitting in the armchair which he's drawn up close to my bed. The infection that I'm suffering from has become uncontrollable, and the antibiotics can't fight it any longer. I'm quite clear about the desperate state of my body, and yet, curiously, this certainty doesn't frighten me. I've learnt a lot in these last months, and I'm now reaping the reward. "James, could you go and see if Luke is there? I'd like to say goodbye to him."

"I'll go," he says, making for the door. He comes back soon afterwards. "He's in the cafeteria, Agnes has just called him, he's coming." I let myself drift into a light sleep while remaining aware. This isn't yet the moment to let myself go completely.

I emerge from a sort of semi-consciousness when Luke hurriedly opens the door of my room. He is slightly out of breath. "There is no need to run," I say smiling, "I'm not going to die right now." James has just left the room, and Luke sits near me patting my hand as he often does, we have our habits... "How are you?" he asks me. The question is absurd, without really being so. "I'm better," I say, "I'm not frightened anymore." The only thing that counts now is my state of mind, it can no longer be any question of my body, we both know that. "I don't know what to say," Luke adds with that distressed little smile I like so much. "It doesn't matter," I reply, "I'd just like you to stay with me for a little while."

"I'm pleased you sent for me; I'd have been very sad not to have seen you anymore."

"Me too, I'd have been sad." I feel good with him and a feeling of peace comes over me. I shut my eyes and I'm very tempted to let go, but time is short and I make a superhuman effort to open my eyes and come back to reality. "Luke, could you please call my parents and James, it's almost time." His eyes fill with tears and he looks at me tenderly. "You're an extraordinary girl," he says in a hoarse voice. "I know," I answer with a smile and I let his look enter my heart. "Please go quickly," I say, because I know that if he doesn't leave my room at once, I shan't be able to let him go... He squeezes my hand very hard and goes towards the door quickly, without turning round.

Shortly afterwards my parents come into my room with James. "Don't cry, Mum, we'll see one another again," I say softly, seeing her face distorted with grief. Her suffering is so great that I can feel it physically as if it had become flesh. "Do you really think that?" she asks, torn between incredulity and the desire to believe. I have the impression that we're no longer mother and daughter, but two human beings facing the same ultimate trial. "Oh yes, Mum, I do believe it," I answer, smiling, "At the beginning it was only a guess, but now it's become much more than that."

James is sitting beside me. He looks deep into my eyes and I get the impression that the light that illuminates him comes into me. What it arouses is very different from the emotions that Luke's eyes waken in me. With James it's something less intimate and more universal. I know he isn't at all frightened by my approaching death. Quite simply, he's come to help me cross over. My parents are sitting at the other side of my bed. We've reached the end of our mutual story. Like me they're exhausted. The last glimmer of hope which gave them the strength to go on has been extinguished from their eyes. It's time for it all to end, no one can go any further. James tells them gently, "You must let her go, she's only waiting for a sign from you to fly away."

"No!" exclaims Mum, and her cry reaches my very heart. I love her so much; I would have wanted her to be happy. Dad gives a gasp that lengthens into a sob, and he buries his face in my shoulder. He lifts me up and holds me to him, as if by doing so he could anchor me to the world forever. Violent sobs shake his body and reverberate into mine. We remain like this for a long time, and finally he puts me gently back on to my bed. I cry with them, more for them than for me.

I can feel myself sliding towards the night, like that day on the island of Zakynthos when I was on the point of fainting after having lost so much blood. The misfortune came with the blood, and I shall die because of the blood. It's my destiny. I know I have only very little time left, but I don't want to leave my parents in grief. "I want James to tell you what he experienced when he was in cardiac arrest," I say to my parents who have just wiped their eyes, and are trying to smile at me. "Listen to him carefully, I'm going to have a little rest in the meantime." I trust him because if there's a single person in the world who can help them, it's him. I hear him starting his story in his warm, steady voice, and I close my eyes. I enter a state of semi-consciousness out of which I emerge from time to time. James is still talking. The sun has just gone down and is setting the sky on fire with a blood red light so brilliant and so magnificent that I'm reconciled with this colour which for me symbolizes so much suffering. I can hear James's words, and I feel reassured. My parents are listening to him attentively. They want to believe him, that's for sure, but I detect in their eyes, beyond the need for comfort, a real conviction born of his testimony, so sincere and so humble. I smile at James who is lost in his memories, trying so hard to help my parents, to describe and explain as fully as he can. If he is physically close, he is at the same time very far from us, communing with this light he carries in his memory and in his heart. Yes, the message has been passed on. I can feel the harmony uniting us, and I realize with relief that my parents will be able to go on their way without me. They will certainly think of me every day, and continue to love me dearly till their last breath, but they will, nevertheless, be able to live without me. The magic of James's words has reunited us again in a common perspective. The idea of death no longer separates us, now we can all wait for it together. Dad smiles at me. I can see the infinite sadness in his eyes and I can feel him struggling inside trying not to let himself be overcome with grief so he can pass on to me all the strength he has left. "Don't be afraid, my love," Mum tells me as she strokes my cheek, "We are to be with you, everything will be alright." A great feeling of calm has filled my hospital room. A perfect communion draws us together beyond the limits of my poor broken-down body, beyond all our bodies. The way has been endlessly long and terribly difficult, strewn with intense anguish and dashed hopes. Angel, the messenger from my future home, was right, yes, she was right when she said that it's the idea of death that is terrifying, but not the passing itself.

I feel within myself so much serenity that I'm letting myself slide into the gentleness of the night that is waiting for me. I go in and out of a state of unconsciousness following the rhythm of my body which is reaching the end of its journey. I stay for a long time in this peaceful state, surrounded by my parents who are at last ready to let me go. In their eyes I can read the immense love they feel for me and I can detect there more hope than resignation, as if a new horizon had opened up for them. I tell myself that I'm very lucky to be able to die in such perfect company. I'm letting myself go, ready to set off in harmony for Angel's land when I see Grandma coming towards me with open arms as a sign of welcome and affection. She is full of joy and much prettier than the day she died. "Come on, my dear," she says with great gentleness, "We're waiting for you."

"I'm coming, Grandma," I reply, overwhelmed with such great happiness, "I'm coming straight away, I just need time to say goodbye to my parents and James."

I open my eyes and I sit up on my bed without pain and without effort. For more than a week now my extreme weakness has prevented me from getting up and even sitting up in my bed, so this movement causes my parents great astonishment. "Are you better, my angel?" asks Mum, in amazement, "Can you sit up?"

"Yes, Mum, I'm very well, I've just seen Grandma who has come to fetch me. She's waiting for me, I'm glad to go with her." My words don't frighten them, they comfort them, I can see that. We have gone beyond belief and mistrust; we have reached the realm of love which leaves no place for doubt.

My parents embrace me and I hold Angel tightly to me. What happiness to be going to join Grandma in such perfect conditions. I can let myself go, I'm no longer afraid of anything, I'm ready for the journey. I tell myself that since Grandma has come to fetch me, it means I have won my wager.

I know the love I feel for my parents won't be lost, but will be sublimated in that place where I'm going. James has told me about this absolute love that he knew, but I wasn't really sure I understood. Now I know exactly what he meant, it is quite simple: the only thing that counts is love, and it lasts forever. If only I had known that it's so easy and so wonderful to die, I would never have been worried for a moment when my leukaemia was diagnosed. But the knowledge that I have today is of course the fruit of my path of suffering and apprenticeship. I have hoped for a long time that the joy of being cured would repair the injustice of my illness, but today I know that the real reward is the blessing that I'm receiving at this precise moment.

"Dad, Mum, I can see the light..."

Books by the author
In English/translated into English

Elsaesser, E. (in press) *Spontaneous Contacts with the Deceased: A large-scale international survey reveals the circumstances, lived experience and beneficial impact of After-Death Communications (ADCs)*, John Hunt Publishing – IFF Books (Specialist and Academic Imprint), Old Alresford, UK.

Ring, K., Elsaesser, E. (2000, Reprint 2006) *Lessons from the Light: What we can learn from the Near-Death Experience*, Moment Point Press, Portsmouth, New Hampshire, USA.

Elsaesser, E. (1997) *On the Other Side of Life: Exploring the Phenomenon of the Near-Death Experience*, Insight Books Plenum Press/Perseus, New York, London.

The author's other books, book chapters and papers in several languages are available on her website:
https://www.evelyn-elsaesser.com/books/

Publications resulting from the research project on After-Death Communications (ADCs)

Elsaesser, E. (2022). *Contactos espontáneos con un fallecido*. Ediciones Urano/Kepler, Madrid, Spain. Original title: Contacts spontanés avec un défunt.

Elsaesser, E. (2021). *Contacts spontanés avec un défunt: Une enquête scientifique atteste la réalité des VSCD*, Editions Exergue, Paris, France.

Elsaesser, E., Roe, C.A., Cooper, C.E., Lorimer, D. (2022). Phänomenologie und Auswirkungen von spontanen Nachtod-Kontakten (NTK) – Forschungsergebnisse und Fallstudien. *Journal of Anomalistics / Zeitschrift für Anomalistik, Band 22 (2022)*, S. 36–71 http://dx.doi.org/10.23793/zfa.2022.36.

Elsaesser, E. (2021). *Spontane Kontakte mit Verstorbenen: Eine wissenschaftliche Untersuchung bestätigt die Realität von Nachtod-Kontakten.* Crotona Verlag, Amerang, Germany. Original title: Contacts spontanés avec un défunt.

Elsaesser, E., Roe, C.A., Cooper, C.E., & Lorimer, D. (2021). The phenomenology and impact of hallucinations concerning the deceased. *BJPsychOpen.*, *Volume 7, Issue 5*, September 2021, e148 DOI: https://doi.org/10.1192/bjo.2021.960

Evrard, R., Dollander, M., Elsaesser, E., Roe, C. A., Cooper, C.E., Lorimer, D. (2021). Exceptional necrophanic experiences and paradoxical mourning: studies of the phenomenology and the repercussions of frightening experiences of contact with the deceased. *Evolution Psychiatrique. Volume 86, Issue 4*, November 2021, Pages e1-e24 https://doi.org/10.1016/j.evopsy.2021.09.001

Evrard, R., Dollander, M., Elsaesser, E., Roe, C. A., Cooper, C.E., Lorimer, D. (2021). Expériences exceptionnelles nécrophaniques et deuil paradoxal: études de la phénoménologie et des répercussions des vécus effrayants de contact avec les défunts. *Evolution Psychiatrique. 86(4)*, pp. 799–824. https://doi.org/10.1016/j.evopsy.2021.05.002

Penberthy, J.K., Pehlivanova, M., Kalelioglu, T. Roe, C.A., Cooper, C.E., Lorimer, D. & Elsaesser, E. (2021). Factors Moderating the Impact of After Death Communications on Beliefs and Spirituality, *OMEGA: Journal of Death & Dying.* July 9, 2021 DOI: 10.1177/00302228211029160

Woollacott, M., Roe, C.A., Cooper, C.E., Lorimer, D., Elsaesser, E. (2021). Perceptual Phenomena Associated with Spontaneous After-Death Communications: Analysis of visual, tactile, auditory and olfactory sensations. *Explore: The Journal of Science and Healing, 17/3.* DOI: 10.1016/j.explore.2021.02.006

All publications of the ADC research project are accessible on the project website: www.adcrp.org/

ROUNDFIRE
BOOKS

FICTION

Historical fiction that lives

Put simply, we publish great stories. Whether it's literary or
popular, a gentle tale or a pulsating thriller, the connecting theme
in all Roundfire fiction titles is that once you pick them up you
won't want to put them down.
If you have enjoyed this book, why not tell other readers by
posting a review on your preferred book site.

Recent bestsellers from Roundfire are:

The Bookseller's Sonnets
Andi Rosenthal

The Bookseller's Sonnets intertwines three love stories with a tale of religious identity and mystery spanning five hundred years and three countries.

Paperback: 978-1-84694-342-3 ebook: 978-184694-626-4

Birds of the Nile
An Egyptian Adventure

N.E. David

Ex-diplomat Michael Blake wanted a quiet birding trip up the Nile – he wasn't expecting a revolution.

Paperback: 978-1-78279-158-4 ebook: 978-1-78279-157-7

Blood Profit$
The Lithium Conspiracy

J. Victor Tomaszek, James N. Patrick, Sr.

The blood of the many for the profits of the few... *Blood Profit$* will take you into the cigar-smoke-filled room where American policy and laws are really made.

Paperback: 978-1-78279-483-7 ebook: 978-1-78279-277-2

The Burden
A Family Saga

N.E. David

Frank will do anything to keep his mother and father apart. But he's carrying baggage – and it might just weigh him down ...

Paperback: 978-1-78279-936-8 ebook: 978-1-78279-937-5

The Cause
Roderick Vincent
The second American Revolution will be a fire lit from
an internal spark.

Paperback: 978-1-78279-763-0 ebook: 978-1-78279-762-3

Don't Drink and Fly
The Story of Bernice O'Hanlon: Part One
Cathie Devitt
Bernice is a witch living in Glasgow. She loses her way in her
life and wanders off the beaten track looking for the garden of
enlightenment.

Paperback: 978-1-78279-016-7 ebook: 978-1-78279-015-0

Gag
Melissa Unger
One rainy afternoon in a Brooklyn diner, Peter Howland
punctures an egg with his fork. Repulsed, Peter pushes the
plate away and never eats again.

Paperback: 978-1-78279-564-3 ebook: 978-1-78279-563-6

The Master Yeshua
The Undiscovered Gospel of Joseph
Joyce Luck
Jesus is not who you think he is. The year is 75 CE. Joseph
ben Jude is frail and ailing, but he has a prophecy to fulfi l ...

Paperback: 978-1-78279-974-0 ebook: 978-1-78279-975-7

On the Far Side, There's a Boy
Paula Coston

Martine Haslett, a thirty-something 1980s woman, plays hard on the fringes of the London drag club scene until one night which prompts her to sign up to a charity. She writes to a young Sri Lankan boy, with consequences far and long.

Paperback: 978-1-78279-574-2 ebook: 978-1-78279-573-5

Tuareg
Alberto Vazquez-Figueroa

With over 5 million copies sold worldwide, *Tuareg* is a classic adventure story from best-selling author Alberto Vazquez-Figueroa, about honour, revenge and a clash of cultures.

Paperback: 978-1-84694-192-4

Readers of ebooks can buy or view any of these bestsellers by clicking on the live link in the title. Most titles are published in paperback and as an ebook. Paperbacks are available in traditional bookshops. Both print and ebook formats are available online.

Find more titles and sign up to our readers' newslett er at http://www.johnhuntpublishing.com/fiction

Follow us on Facebook at https://www.facebook.com/ JHPfiction and Twitter at https://twitter.com/JHPFiction